The Poisoned Pink Punch

A Witch's Cove Mystery
Book 10

Vella Day

Death by poison is not a good way to go—unless the punch tastes good.

My ten-year high school reunion was supposed to be fun—seeing old friends and maybe even making a few new ones. And I was really looking forward to spending an evening with Jaxson's brother, Drake, again. Too bad, when we entered the dance, one of Drake's friends was lying dead on the floor covered in pink punch.

Sure Kyle Covington was a very rich investor who'd made his share of enemies, but had any of them been at the reunion?

Considering Drake's connection with the deceased, what kind of friend would I be if I didn't do some investigating? After all, I knew most of the suspects. Out of the blue, an unexpected arrival joins forces with Drake—one with magic. Was she involved in the murder or would she help solve the case?

If you want to check up on the status of our crime solving, I'll either be slurping down a chocolate shake at the Spellbound Diner or chatting with my aunt at the Tiki Hut Grill. Don't worry—Jaxson and Iggy will also be on the case.

Chapter One

DRAKE HARRISON KNOCKED on my bedroom door. "You've been in there a long time, Glinda."

Both Jaxson Harrison, my partner in the Pink Iguana Sleuths' Agency, and his brother, Drake, were waiting in my living room, but only Drake and I were going to our tenth high school reunion. Jaxson's tenth reunion had been six years ago, and he honestly thought he might be a buzz kill if he went with us. As hard as it would be to spend an evening without him, I didn't want to put him out. I know he didn't think highly of his high school days.

"I'm almost ready." I checked my image in the mirror once more. I'd already changed my outfit three times. Enough was enough. Impressing others might have been my MO in high school, but no longer. I was a respected business owner now. It didn't matter—or at least it shouldn't matter—what my old high school friends thought of me.

Inhaling, I pushed open the door, lifted my arms in the air, and twirled around. "Ta-da!"

Jaxson whistled. "Maybe I should come with you guys after all, so I can fend off the men."

I laughed. I adored him for thinking I looked good. "You don't think everyone will be disappointed that I'm not dressed in all pink?"

"What are you talking about? You have on a pink blouse and pink earrings."

I plucked the black skirt from my legs. "Hel-lo!"

Drake rolled his eyes at his brother. "I'm glad you're the one who has to deal with her every day."

"Now, you're just being mean. Admittedly, I usually only wear my pink signature color, but I can handle some variety now and again."

Iggy, my pink iguana familiar, poked his head out from under the sofa. "Can I come with you?"

"To the reunion? Why?"

"Where you go, disaster often follows," he said.

"That is not true—at least not all of the time." I looked over at Jaxson for some help.

He stepped over to Iggy and picked him up. "I thought you wanted to spend the evening with me, buddy. We were going to watch some TV."

"I guess that would be okay. Can I ask Aimee to come over?" Aimee was my aunt's cat who lived across the hallway from us. Aimee, like Iggy, could talk.

"Sure." He placed Iggy on the sofa, and then Jaxson hugged me. "Have a good time, but watch out for Drake. He can be unruly at times."

I chuckled. That was the furthest thing from the truth. Jaxson had always been the troubled older brother. "Don't worry. I'll make sure he doesn't step out of line."

Drake touched my arm. "Come on. We're already late."

Who wanted to be the first to arrive at a party anyway? Oh, yeah. Drake did. I stood on my tiptoes and kissed Jaxson goodbye. "You don't have to babysit the animal, you know."

He grinned. "I know."

"Who are you calling an animal?" Iggy huffed.

"Behave for Jaxson." I wagged a finger at him, though I had no doubt the two of them would have a good time—or at least Iggy would. He adored my boyfriend.

After Iggy assured me he'd behave, Drake and I headed downstairs. Being the gentleman that he was, Drake insisted he chauffeur me the three miles to the high school.

Rihanna, my eighteen-year old cousin, had volunteered to head the party's decoration committee. She, along with her two new girlfriends, Casi and Lena, promised to make it an evening to remember. I hoped that meant the theme would include some pink.

Drake glanced over at me. "Are you nervous?"

I knew why he asked. I often obsessed over things. "Surprisingly, no. I have a successful business, a boyfriend, and a drop-dead gorgeous escort for the night." I'd heard that being unattached at one of these reunions was a big no-no. Or at least for women it seemed to be.

He chuckled. "Thanks. I don't say it often enough, but I'm proud of all you've accomplished since high school."

"Aw, thank you, but look at you. You've done even better."

"Maybe, but it has come at a cost. I've been so consumed making my cheese and wine shop a success that I've barely had time to date. Not to mention, I've missed our little talks," he said.

"Me, too, but we can blame that on Jaxson." His brother had been helping Drake with inventory and such until Jaxson and I teamed up to open our sleuth agency, which meant Drake had to pick up the slack. Thankfully, he'd recently found more part-time help.

Drake laughed. "Let's do that. As his penance, my brother needs to give you up at least twice a month so the two of us can create our ice cream sundae masterpieces."

"I love doing that with you." I twisted toward him. "How did a health nut end up being your brother?"

He shook his head. "Some mysteries will never be solved."

Before we could decide how the two brothers could be so different, we arrived at the school parking lot. The flashing sheriff's car lights shot my senses to high alert. "What are Steve and Nash doing here? I can't imagine our class is that rowdy."

Drake parked. "Let's see what's going on."

When we reached the double doors that led into the gym, Nash Solano, our deputy, blocked our way. "Glinda. Drake. I'm afraid there's been an incident. Steve asked I keep out all new arrivals."

"What kind of incident are we talking about?" I was fairly confident that we could talk our way inside. I'd saved Nash's life recently, and he owed us.

"Someone died."

I sucked in a body-trembling breath. "Who was it?"

He checked his notepad. "A Kyle Covington."

Drake grabbed my arm. "Kyle? You have to be kidding."

"I take it you knew him?" Nash asked.

"Yes. We were on the debate and wrestling teams together and were good friends."

Nash looked over at me. "Since I know Glinda will worm

her way into this investigation at some point, I'll let you guys through, but don't touch anything—especially you, Glinda. If you spot anyone who might have a motive for wanting this man dead, please let us know."

I might have been offended that he thought I'd *worm* my way into an investigation, but since this was a friend of Drake's, I had to help, and Nash knew that. "I guess this means he was murdered?"

"I spoke too soon. I've been assigned door duty, that's all, but Steve might have more information."

That was a line if ever I'd heard one, but we'd find out the truth soon enough. As we entered the gym that had a rather festive blue and black decor with a splash of pink thrown in for good measure, I couldn't help but experience a trickle of excitement. It was totally uncalled for and inappropriate at a time like this, but it was a bit thrilling to be allowed into a murder scene for a change—assuming Kyle had been killed.

A surprising number of people were there, which suggested Steve had asked all those present to stay around so he could question them. Even if the sheriff didn't know for sure Kyle had been killed, he might have wanted to cover his bases in case it turned out to be the case.

I spotted my cousin Rihanna off to the side, huddled with her two new girlfriends, and we headed toward them.

Hopefully, one of them saw what happened. For sure, Steve wouldn't share what he'd learned—at least not until the medical examiner gave him her report.

"Rihanna, what is going on?" I asked.

"Glinda. I'm so glad you're here. I don't know much other than a few minutes after Casi and Lena had delivered the punch bowl to the main table, someone started screaming that a man had collapsed."

"Did either of you girls see anything?"

Lena shook her head, and Casi ran her palms down her skirt. "Sort of. After I heard the punchbowl crash to the ground, I turned around and saw some guy lying there. I think he died like right away," Casi reported. "But I didn't see anyone near him or anything."

"How terrible for you to witness that."

She nodded. Since my parents owned the funeral home in town, I was used to dead bodies, but this girl wouldn't be, especially at her age.

Drake touched my arm. "I'm going over there to make sure it really is Kyle."

"Sure." I understood his need to be certain there hadn't been a mistake. I'd never had a friend my age die, and I couldn't imagine what that would be like. I turned back to the girls. "Did the sheriff say everyone had to remain in the gym until he'd questioned them?" That's what he'd done at our Halloween party when my Aunt Fern's boyfriend had been killed.

"Yes," Lena said.

Just then our medical examiner and her son—who happened to be Rihanna's boyfriend—arrived. I expected my cousin to dart over to him, but she remained where she was. Gavin must have told her that when he was working a crime scene she needed to stay back.

"Did you know the dead guy, too?" Casi asked.

"A little. I mean, Drake and I were the ones who were close. Only because he and Kyle were good friends did we talk sometimes." I had to search my mind for when we'd interacted other than when I was with Drake. Ten years was a long time. "Kyle and I had a couple of math classes together, but he mostly kept to himself. Back then, I was trying to figure out how to fit in, and I wasn't looking for a boyfriend or anything. Even then, I could tell Kyle was destined to do great things. The guy was a genius."

Drake returned. From the vacant look in his eyes, it was not good news. "It's Kyle. I can't believe it."

I hugged him. "I'm sorry, Drake."

"Thanks." He shook his head. "I couldn't see any evidence of murder. It appears as if he drank the punch, had some kind of reaction—or maybe even a heart attack—and then knocked over the bowl as he collapsed. There's pink punch everywhere."

"Good thing time of death was known. Otherwise, the cold punch might have affected his core body temperature."

Drake dipped his chin. "Glinda."

Dang it. I was being too clinical and not a sympathetic friend. It was the way I often coped with tragedy. "Sorry. Did Steve say anything?"

"What could he say other than he could tell I was upset? Mr. Vincent is taking names and asking questions."

I craned my neck and spotted our principal. "That's smart of Steve to ask him to take roll. Mr. Vincent might be old, but the man never forgets a student. If Steve had spoken to everyone, someone might have lied about their identity."

"If I'd put something in the punch," Lena said, "I wouldn't give my real name."

The punch being spiked with poison was a good theory,

but only if Kyle had been the only one who drank from it. Because no one else appeared ill, it wasn't clear what had happened. "I'm sure many would do the same, but Mr. Vincent will spot the liars."

Drake clasped my arm. "As long as we're here, we should mingle."

Now it was my turn to dip my chin. "You want to catch up with old friends?" That wasn't like him.

"No. I want to see who's here. Kyle wasn't the most liked guy in the school, if you recall."

I shrugged. "I think I was too into my pink clothing and my studies to have noticed." Not to mention my magic.

"Assuming he didn't die of a heart attack or some other natural cause, who are you thinking might have wanted him dead?" Rihanna asked.

My cousin would make a great sleuth one day. Okay, to be fair, she already was a pretty good one. Rihanna could not only read minds—at least most of the time—she could connect the dots when others often couldn't.

"His death could be from natural causes, but Kyle still looked fit," Drake said. "To be honest, we lost touch a few years back after one of his online trading schemes hit it big."

"Trading, as in stock trading?" That was fascinating. With my math background, I probably would have done quite well in that field had I pursued it.

"Yes, but then he got into cryptocurrencies—Bitcoin, I think—along with a few Alt coins. He invested when those coins cost pennies. Then the price skyrocketed, and he became mega rich, or so I read."

"That might have upset a few people."

Drake looked around. "True, but none of those people would be at our ten-year high school reunion."

"I wouldn't be too sure. Jealousy can cut deep, and those kinds of people can be creative. Admittedly, holding a grudge for ten years seems remote," I said.

"I won't discount anything. Kyle won a lot of debate tournaments during his high school career. The last one allowed him to compete at States—which he won."

The memories rushed back. "If I recall, that resulted in him receiving a full ride to Harvard. I bet whoever came in second might be angry at that lost opportunity."

"I suppose," Drake said. "The first runner up was Ronnie Taggert who ended up at Florida State. I don't know how he fared after that."

"Where did Kyle end up after college?" I asked.

"Last I heard, he was working in Silicon Valley."

That was so far from my world, I couldn't even imagine living in the technological fast lane. "Good for him. Did he ever marry?"

"Not that I was aware, but as I said, we lost touch a few years back."

"I can subtly find out about his marital status," Rihanna said.

I loved her enthusiasm. "That's okay. We'll find out sooner or later."

A tall redhead made a beeline toward us, looking as if she was on a mission. The beautiful woman appeared familiar, but I couldn't place her.

When she reached us, she broke into a dazzling smile. "Drake Harrison, is that really you?"

My protective instincts shot up, even though he and I were just friends. Drake spun to face her. "Yes?"

At least that made two of us who didn't know her.

"It's me. Andorra Leyton."

Drake's mouth gaped open. He then dragged his gaze from her head to her toes and back again. Okay, clearly, he was impressed. "Andi? I can't believe it's you. You've changed."

She chuckled. "I hope for the better. Braces and glasses weren't a real good look for me back then."

"Ah, yeah. Definitely for the better." Drake all but drooled.

Once they finished hugging, I should have said something, but I, too, was in shock over her transformation. Andorra and I had only briefly interacted in high school. She'd mentioned she had some witch talents, but it wasn't something I wanted to explore at the time. Being a seventeen-year-old math geek made me enough of an outsider. I didn't need people learning about my abilities—limited as they were.

If I remembered correctly, Andorra Leyton had a crush on Drake, but back then, he was either too focused on his studies, going to wrestling practice, or working on his debate skills, to give her the time of day.

Andorra faced me. "Is that you, Glinda?"

Expect for maybe a few added pounds, I hadn't changed all that much—or so I thought. "It sure is."

Before I could decide if I was happy to see her or not, she hugged me too. Okay, that was unexpected. Andorra leaned back. "You look amazing. And the black skirt suits you."

Maybe she wasn't so bad after all. She smiled and then

turned back to Drake. "I'm so sorry about Kyle. Is it a shock or what?"

"It's horrible," he said. "I still haven't wrapped my head around it. Did you hear anything?"

"As a matter of fact, I did."

Her words perked me up. "What did you find out?"

Chapter Two

"I JUST SPOKE with Patricia Diaz, who, if you didn't know, is now Patricia Haltern."

Memories of Kyle with Patricia making out under the football stadium bleachers rushed back to me. "I remember how devastated she was after Kyle dumped her at the end of their senior year."

"He had no choice. Kyle was headed to Harvard, and it wasn't like she could follow him there," Andorra said.

"True, but I'm sure it hurt anyway." I looked around to see if I could spot Patricia, but I didn't see her. Either she'd changed a lot or she was sitting down.

"I know it did. Patricia and I kept in touch until she married Harry, who, by the way, isn't the nicest person in the world. He insisted Patricia not contact me again."

"Ouch." Nothing was worse than marrying someone who didn't give you the respect you deserved. "Did her husband come with her tonight?"

"I saw her talking with some man who I assume was him. I've never met Harry, though."

"Do you think either of them could have wanted Kyle dead, assuming Kyle was murdered?" Drake asked.

Andorra shrugged. "We all had crushes ten years ago.

Some worked out and some didn't. Was it enough to want to kill a person? I don't know."

Just then two men who worked part-time at the morgue pushed a gurney with Kyle's body on it out of the gym. "I'm hoping Dr. Sanchez learns the cause of Kyle's death sooner rather than later."

Drake nodded to my necklace. "Do you think you could pass your stone over the punchbowl to see if it was poisoned?"

Poison was a logical killing agent. "I don't think it works that way. So far, my necklace has only responded to bodies, parts of bodies, or evil warlocks."

Andorra held up a finger. "My cousin said you stopped by the Hex and Bones shop a while back asking about a rather strong potion. How did that work out?"

I kept forgetting that Andorra and Elizabeth were related. "Great. It did exactly as planned. And more so."

"That's fantastic."

A man about our age came up to Casi. "The sheriff said we can go." His gruff and rather insensitive comment made my skin crawl.

She stiffened for a moment. "Okay." She turned to Rihanna and Lena and hugged them both. "Call me if you learn anything. Okay?"

"Sure," Lena said.

"Was that Christian Durango?" I asked after they left.

"It was. He hasn't become any more charming, has he?" Andorra said.

"No." I planned to ask Rihanna about him when she wasn't with Lena. Casi might have mentioned what he was up to these days. I knew he lived on the outskirts of town, but I never ran into him.

Unless I got my signals crossed, Casi had witch powers, which implied her older brother was a warlock. Back in the day, I didn't ask about those things. The last murder case we worked on involved death by witchcraft. Could that be what had happened here?

"Since people are allowed to leave, is anyone up for an ice cream sundae at Beaches?" Drake might be trying to end the night on a positive note.

"I love that idea." I turned to Rihanna and Lena. "Do you girls want to join us?"

"I would," Lena said, "but I told my mom I'd be home as soon as we finished decorating, and I'm already late."

"I'm sure she'll understand why you were delayed. Another time then." Since Rihanna's boyfriend would be busy for the next few hours helping his mom with Kyle's body, my cousin would be free—unless she didn't want to spend her evening with us old folks.

"I'm in," Rihanna said.

"Great. The more the merrier." Besides, she might be able to learn what Andorra was really thinking.

Drake turned to Andorra. "You are coming, right?"

She grinned. "I wouldn't miss it for the world. I haven't been to the ice cream shop since before we graduated."

I placed a friendly hand on her arm. "Trust me, it looks the same, only a bit more rundown. Personally, I find it's more charming that way."

"I'm looking forward to it. The last time I came back was for Mom's funeral, and I wasn't up for stopping in."

"I'm sorry about your mom." I still couldn't believe I was

unaware that Andorra's mom was Bertha Murdoch's daughter, but in all fairness, I wasn't in Witch's Cove at the time of her death.

"Thanks."

Drake faced me. "Why don't you call Jaxson and see if he wants to join us."

"That's a great idea. I'm sure he will want to. But first, I want to speak with Steve." I wanted to assure him we will help with the case in any capacity we can.

Our sheriff was with our principal, but when he saw me, he stepped away from Mr. Vincent. "Did you learn anything?"

I didn't expect that question since I wasn't used to him asking my opinion at the start of an investigation. "Not a lot, but Andorra Leyton has been chatting with possible suspects. Drake, Jaxson, Rihanna, and I are going over to the ice cream shop with her right now, and I'll be sure to pick her brain. I'll let you know If I learn anything."

Steve tossed back a brief smile. "You do that."

Once I gave my best to Mr. Vincent, I returned to Drake and Andorra. Even though Rihanna was with us, I kind of felt like a third wheel. I'm sure this was what Drake often experienced when Jaxson and I started our company together.

"Ready?" he asked. I nodded.

"I drove, so I'll meet you there," Andorra said.

"Me, too," Rihanna responded.

On the way out, I called Jaxson who said he would be happy to join us and that he'd save us a table if he got to the ice cream shop first.

"Good idea. I bet the place will be packed now that the reunion has been canceled."

"Good point."

I disconnected just as Drake started the engine.

"What do you think of Andorra?" he asked.

"Think?" I wasn't sure what he wanted me to say.

"She's grown up, wouldn't you say?"

I chuckled. "So have you."

He shrugged. "I suppose."

While Jaxson was taller and a bit more fit than Drake, they both were very handsome men. They had also both improved with age, which was so not fair. "More importantly, what are your thoughts about her?"

"That I was a fool in high school not to have gone after her. Andorra had made it obvious that she was interested."

If she had an ulterior motive for cozying up to him now, I didn't want to see him hurt. "Are you certain she's not married?"

He slowed the car. "No, I'm not sure, but since she flirted a lot, I figured she wasn't. Hopefully, that tidbit of information will come out in the next few minutes, especially if it becomes obvious that you're with my brother and not me."

Ah, so that was why he wanted me to have Jaxson meet us. It made sense. Personally, I was there to learn what she knew. If she was Bertha Murdoch's granddaughter, she'd have some powerful witch genes inside of her—ones that might be helpful in solving this case. And yes, I know, we might not even have a case, but twenty-seven-year-olds didn't just drop dead without a good reason.

We parked in front of the ice cream shop close to Jaxson's car. A few seconds later, both Andorra and Rihanna pulled alongside of us. "I hope Jaxson didn't have too hard of a time convincing Iggy that he needed to stay home," I said.

"I thought Iggy didn't like cold places."

"He doesn't, but being left out of the loop is difficult for him. Most likely my poor iguana will be in a foul mood when I return."

"No one likes to be left out."

His sincerity made me feel guilty for not including Drake more often in our investigations, especially since he was smart and level-headed. Now that he had help with his store, we would consult him more.

When we entered, I searched the packed place. Thankfully, Jaxson had managed to snag one of the two large tables. He spotted us, stood, and smiled. As soon as we reached him, Jaxson leaned over and kissed me. I didn't look at Andorra as I wasn't sure what she thought my relationship with Drake had been. Hopefully, she now understood we were just friends.

"Jaxson," Drake said. "This is Andorra Leyton."

Jaxson held out a hand. "Nice to meet you. Since I haven't seen you around, I take it you aren't currently living in Witch's Cove?"

"No, right after I graduated from college, I moved to New York City where I got a job at a publishing house."

"That sounds like fun." I meant it.

"It was at first, but with the economy the way it is, it became a pressure cooker, so I quit."

Drake's eyes widened. "Will you be returning to New York?"

I swear he was holding his breath. Why he was so drawn to her, I didn't know. Then again, Drake had put his business first for so long, he might have decided now was the time to settle down. He certainly could do worse that Andorra Leyton—or at least I thought that at the moment. I hope she wasn't some wolf in sheep's clothing, looking for a handout. While Drake was holding his own financially, he certainly didn't live a lavish lifestyle.

"Actually, I think I might stay in Witch's Cove."

I hadn't seen that coming. "What would you do? I don't think we even have any authors in this town."

She smiled. "No. I'm done with my publishing life. My grandmother is getting on in age, and Elizabeth and I have been talking about running the Hex and Bones Apothecary ourselves."

Wow. We needed some young blood in the witch community. "That would be great."

"No kids along the way?" Drake asked—clearly not caring about being subtle or learning about her plans for any improvements she might have in mind for the occult store.

"No, you?"

"Haven't had time. I've been busy running my wine and cheese shop."

Andorra smiled. "Oh, wow. You always talked about doing that in high school."

Jaxson pushed back his chair. "I'm ordering my ice cream. Anyone care to join me?"

Did seeing a woman flirt with his brother make Jaxson uncomfortable? Though his response could be something as simple as wanting some dessert. With so many people, the service staff wasn't prepared to take our order at the table, which meant we needed to go to the counter and pick out something.

"I'm game." For me, the choice was easy—a scoop of mint chocolate chip and a scoop of chocolate. Since this was like a date, I added some chocolate sauce and sprinkles. Once we all had our dessert in hand, we returned to the table.

"Drake, Glinda mentioned one of your friends died on the gym floor," Jaxson said. "I'm so sorry."

"Thanks. I still can't believe Kyle Covington is gone."

Jaxson shook his head. "The name doesn't ring a bell."

Drake gave him a rundown how they knew each other. It made sense Jaxson wouldn't have known Kyle. By the time Drake and I were in high school, Jaxson was off doing his thing away from Witch's Cove.

"And you think he was murdered?" He looked from Drake to me.

"We'll have to wait for the autopsy before we charge into murder mode," I said.

Everyone seemed to think that was for the best. For the next few minutes, we focused on eating our amazingly good tasting dessert. Naturally, I couldn't keep away from discussing the recent events for long. "Drake, I know you and Kyle kind of lost touch, but did you hear if he had a business partner or a demanding boss who might have had a conflict with him?"

"No, but even if I knew of someone, I doubt his life outside of Witch's Cove had any effect on what happened to him tonight."

"Who's to say someone didn't come with him?" Andorra asked.

"I suppose we won't know until after Mr. Vincent turns in the names of those who are not alums," Drake said.

"If it was the killer, I would imagine that person would

have been hovering around our sheriff, trying to learn what Steve had figured out," I said.

Andorra nodded. "Excellent point. The possible killer might also have wrangled an invitation from an alum for the express purpose of being at the reunion when Kyle was here."

"That would make sense." I looked over at Drake. "What do you think?"

"Anything's possible. I say, we keep an open mind."

Andorra lifted her cup of ice cream and scooped out some. "It sounds as if you all have done this kind of thing before."

Now, I had to brag. "Actually, Jaxson and I run the Pink Iguana Sleuths' Agency."

"You're private investigators?" Her eyes widened.

Andorra didn't need to sound so surprised. I had always been a nosy one. "Technically, we're sleuths. We often help our new sheriff with cases, especially if magic is involved." I nodded to Rihanna. "My cousin here is very special. She's been working with Gertrude Poole, learning to improve her mind reading skills."

"Wow. I wish I could do that," Andorra said.

"Don't we all wish that."

We spent the rest of the time talking about Andorra's future plans. "Where are you going to live?" Drake asked.

"With Elizabeth—at least for now—but nothing is set in stone. I guess it depends on how I like it here." She smiled at Drake.

His lips quirked upward. "Then I'll make it my mission to see that you do."

Oh, boy. I'd never seen Drake fall so hard. I hope Andorra hadn't put some kind of love spell on my good friend.

Chapter Three

"WHAT DO YOU think of Andorra?" I asked Jaxson once we'd returned to my apartment.

I wanted him to take me home, mostly to assure me I wasn't blowing things out of proportion about Andorra and Drake.

"She seems lovely. Why?" he asked.

I explained how the moment she spotted Drake, she made a beeline toward him. "Andorra fawned all over him."

"I don't see that as a problem. It's always nice to see an old friend."

I might have been a wee bit jealous over their instant connection. "I guess. On a positive note, before we arrived, Andorra had already started questioning people about Kyle's death."

"Definitely an evil person—a flirt, a friend, and a snoop? You know what I think?"

I wasn't sure I did, considering his tone. "What?"

"You're jealous she might be a good sleuth and secondly, that she might take Drake away from you."

I laughed, though it sounded forced even to me. "I'm not with Drake. We're just friends."

"That's the problem. My brother is the friend who is

always there if you need someone to talk to or have ice cream with. If Andorra comes into his life, where would that leave you?"

"Ouch." I wanted to say he was completely wrong, but I had the sick feeling that he might not be.

Jaxson gathered me in his arms. "It doesn't matter. We have each other."

His words calmed me. "We do. Thank you."

Jaxson looked down at me and smiled. "Do you want to start a list of who might be guilty?"

I leaned back and punched him. "I don't always have to work."

He dipped his chin. "Since when?"

"Fine, but let's start tomorrow. I think I'll be needing input from Drake and Andorra, not to mention the names Mr. Vincent was compiling before my list will be useful."

"Tomorrow it is." Jaxson leaned over and kissed me. "We'll get this person."

Assuming Kyle was murdered, I had to hope we would.

IGGY CAME WITH me to work the next day since he insisted on being in the thick of things. Thankfully, I'd purchased a heating pad for him since the draft in this building was rather bad.

Voices sounded downstairs from Drake's wine and cheese shop, and a moment later, Jaxson's cell rang.

"Yo, bro. What's up?" Jaxson looked over at me. "We can. I get it. No problem." He disconnected. "Drake has requested our presence downstairs. He doesn't want to leave the store, and Trace isn't coming in for another hour."

"I heard a female voice. Is Andorra with him?" After thinking about what Jaxson said last night, I realized I had been a little jealous, and I had no right to be. Drake deserved to be happy—like me.

"She is."

"Good. Andorra is savvy. It will help to put three sets of memories together instead of two."

"I agree. Let's go," Jaxson said.

We'd just said our hellos to the happy couple when my phone rang. "Excuse me." I checked the caller ID. "It's Elissa," I announced with probably too much joy.

"Who is that?" Andorra asked.

"The medical examiner." I swiped the On button. "Hey, Elissa."

"Glinda, I can't believe I'm doing this again, but could you come to the morgue?"

My heart nearly stopped. This was the second time she'd called asking for my help in the last two months. "Of course. Are you thinking magic is involved in Kyle's death?" It was why she'd asked me to get involved the last time.

"Possibly. Kyle was poisoned, but something isn't adding up. I don't want to give you too much information. It might color your findings."

"Of course. I'll head on over now." I disconnected and then told everyone what Elissa said.

"May I come?" Andorra asked.

"I doubt the medical examiner will mind, but it's kind of boring watching me swing my pendant over the body."

Andorra looked to the side and then back at me. "Here's the thing. I have some magical talents that might help."

I knew she was a witch, but I didn't know the extent of her abilities. "Meaning what?"

"If Kyle was poisoned or had a spell put on him, I might be able to detect what was used."

"The actual poison itself?" I could only say if poison had killed the person.

"Yes."

Wow. "That would be awesome."

Andorra smiled. "Let's hope your medical examiner thinks so."

After we told the men we'd hurry back, we went over to the morgue. Once there, I knocked on the closed autopsy door. When Elissa answered, she glanced over at Andorra. It made sense she'd wondered why I'd ask a stranger to join me. "This is Andorra Leyton, a fellow classmate of mine. She has powers that might complement mine."

The good doctor let out a breath and nodded. "Welcome. I'm Doctor Sanchez."

Gavin was inside, and when his brows pinched, I made the introductions again.

"Ah, yes. Rihanna mentioned you." He smiled and held up his gloved hand that was none too clean, letting us know why he couldn't shake ours.

"Shall we get started?" Dr. Sanchez said.

I turned to Andorra. "What do you need?"

"You do your thing, and then I'll do mine."

That worked for me. I removed my pink pendant from around my neck. Like I had done many times before, I swung the diamond back and forth over the body, starting at the feet and moving upward. Because poison was the culprit, I didn't expect to see anything until I reached the stomach, but I was wrong. From the start, the pendant changed from its original pink color to a light yellow.

"Why did it change color?" Andorra asked so softly, I barely heard her.

"Yellow implies magic."

"Magic? That should narrow down the field of suspects. That being said, a spell could have occurred at any time, even before the reunion started."

I didn't want to think about that right now, so I merely nodded. I needed to concentrate.

As my pendant moved closer to the stomach, the diamond became imbued with streaks of purple, which meant poison. I'd never encountered both at the same time before, though. As I went past the stomach toward the heart, the purple color faded, and the yellow intensified.

When I finished, I turned to Elissa. "It looks like Kyle was poisoned with some kind of magic potion. Andorra, what do you think?"

"I don't know what your colors mean, but it is possible. Let me try something."

She placed her hand on Kyle's stomach and closed her eyes. Her breathing slowed, almost as if she was going into some kind of trance. A moment later, she removed her hand and opened her eyes. "There's sage, crenolen root, turmeric, and one or two other ingredients I can't identify."

Elissa sucked in a breath. "That is remarkable. I found the sage and turmeric, but I've yet to do an analysis on the other ingredients. Would those things be something found in a magic spell?"

"I'd like to confer with my cousin and grandmother before I say for sure. I have a feeling Memaw will know."

Memaw? It was hard enough picturing Bertha Murdoch as her grandmother, let alone allowing anyone to call her Memaw, but what did I know? "That sounds awesome." I turned back to Dr. Sanchez. "Will you put poison as the cause of death?"

"Absolutely, but I'll need to narrow it down before I send out the results."

Andorra clasped my arm. "We should see what the sheriff did with the cups."

I was still mentally back on the magical poison. "Cups?"

"Kyle had to drink out of one. I'm wondering if only his drink was tampered with, though it's more likely the sorcerer added the ingredients to the whole bowl."

"If the whole bowl had been tampered with, someone would have complained about the taste. Or are you thinking someone said a spell just as Kyle was drinking the liquid? If not, many people would have died."

"That would make sense," she said. "Those ingredients in and of themselves are not poisonous. It's why he or she could purchase them anywhere—or find them in the woods. Once mixed together, all this person had to do was say a spell, which would turn them into a lethal cocktail."

Horrifyingly simple. "I'm guessing this witch would have said the spell just as Kyle was taking a sip. That meant the person was in the gym at the time, right?" I shivered at that thought.

Andorra placed a hand on my arm. "That is my guess. Let's not make any assumptions yet, but since you're the sleuth, Glinda, I have every faith you'll find this person."

No pressure. "I'll try."

After we thanked Elissa Sanchez, Andorra and I headed back to Drake's store where he and Jaxson were chatting downstairs. My partner looked up. "How did it go?"

I told him what we found out.

Drake whistled. "Some random person put a spell on Kyle, and it killed him? Is that what you're telling us?"

I nodded and then looked over at Andorra to see if she'd add anything.

"That's what I think too," she said.

We both sat down at the table in the back room. "What's the plan?" Drake asked.

"I want to reach out to Patricia Haltern to see if she knows anything," Andorra said.

Really? "That's great, unless she had something to do with Kyle's death. Then she'd keep her mouth shut."

Andorra held up a finger. "I need to mention my other talent."

The woman kept getting better. "Do tell."

"I can touch a person and sense if they've used any of the herbs in the spell recently."

"Color me impressed." I was being totally sincere.

"What if they've washed their hands?" Jaxson said.

"It doesn't matter. The ingredients would have seeped into their bodies through their skin. It will take days to leave. Mind you, if they wore gloves, it won't show."

"Do you think the three of us could come up with a list of

people who might have wanted to harm Kyle? That would expand your audience, Andorra, of who you might want to touch," I said.

"I can help make a list," Drake said. "It won't be complete by any means since I have no idea who Kyle interacted with over the last few years."

I snapped my fingers. "Does the gym have any surveillance cameras by any chance? Someone had to have put the ingredients in either his drink or the punch at some point."

"I'll give the school a call," Jaxson said. "Rihanna might have an idea, too, since she was there."

"Good thinking."

"Is the sheriff doing an analysis of the punch?" Drake asked.

"I imagine he would. We should ask him." I turned to Andorra. "Want to come with me to check it out?"

She smiled. "I'd like nothing better." Drake cleared his throat, and she chuckled. "Other than catching up with Drake."

I was proud of myself for not groaning. "Let's go."

When we entered the sheriff's office, I was happy to see Pearl at her station. She looked up and smiled. "My, oh, my. Andorra, you have grown up."

Hold it! How did she recognize Andorra, and I hadn't? Pearl was almost eighty. Then again, Andorra's grandmother and she were friends. They'd probably shared family photos.

"This is Pearl, the sheriff's grandmother."

Andorra smiled, looking like a professional New York business woman. "Nice to meet you."

We didn't have time for a lot of gossip today. If someone

had killed Kyle, I wouldn't be surprised if this person left town in the near future, if he hadn't already. "Is Steve in? We have some news on the Kyle Covington case."

Her brows rose. "Let me see."

I don't know why she didn't just tell us to go on back to his office. A moment later, she nodded in the direction of his office. I knocked and went in.

"Ah, my resident witches come to visit, I see." He smiled and then extended his hand to Andorra. "We haven't formally met, but I've heard you were working the gym yesterday."

I had mentioned Andorra had been asking questions of possible suspects.

"I was. I'm Andorra Leyton."

"How can I help you, ladies?" Steve sat back down, and we grabbed the two chairs in front of his desk.

I went through my findings, and then how Andorra was able to detect the combination of herbs used. "The yellow glow of my necklace implies witchcraft. Who is responsible is still unknown."

"Except that they'd have to be a witch or a warlock," Steve stated.

"True, though it's possible someone hired a sorcerer to do the spell."

He huffed. "That would throw a wrench into things. Maybe coming to a town called Witch's Cove wasn't my smartest move. The mayor might have been better off with someone who has your talents."

I almost blushed. "We're here to help."

He chuckled. "And you always do. What trouble do you plan to get into next?"

Chapter Four

M E? GET INTO trouble? It wasn't as if the sheriff ever needed to save me from near death. On the contrary, my research had always resulted in bringing the person to justice without any personal harm to me or my family.

"I promise to play it safe," I said. "We just came to see if you've tested the punch for poison—or rather to see if anything unusual was added to the punch."

"I sent a sample to the lab."

"Good." That was all I could ask. Now for the hard part. "By any chance, could we get a list of the people at the reunion?" I held up a hand. "No, I can't tell who might be a witch or a warlock, but I can ask around. If that person went to the Hex and Bones for some ingredients, it would imply they might have magic. Of course, if you'd like to do all of the legwork yourself, be my guest."

Steve smiled and shook his head. "You've learned how to push my buttons, Glinda."

Pride filled me. "I'm trying to be a responsible citizen. Besides, Kyle was a dear friend of Drake's. I knew him, of course, but not that well."

Steve pulled open his drawer and handed me his yellow tablet. "I haven't transcribed this yet."

"May I take a photo of it then?"

"Sure."

There appeared to be about sixty names, and sadly, I didn't recognize many of them. Wanting to be sure all of the images were readable, I took several photos. I then handed the pad back to him. "Anything I should know before I stick my nose into this?"

His shoulders sagged. "Will it matter if I tell you to be careful?"

Our sheriff knew me well. "No, but we'll ask around before confronting anyone. Between Andorra, me, her cousin Elizabeth, and Drake, I bet we can narrow down the field."

"I appreciate learning what you find out."

"As always." Since I'd received what we'd come for, I pushed back my chair and thanked him.

Once we left, I turned to Andorra. "Coffee or tea?"

"Excuse me?"

Andorra had a lot to learn about Witch's Cove. What better place to start indoctrinating her than having her meet the gossip queens? "Do you prefer coffee or tea?"

"Both, but I could go for a hot tea right about now."

"Tea it is."

We went across the street into The Moon Bay Tea Shop where Maude, the owner and resident gossip queen, looked up and smiled. I led Andorra up to the counter and introduced her.

"So, this is Bertha's granddaughter. Well, I'll be."

Naturally, Maude had to ask a few questions before letting us order, but that was okay. These two needed to bond. I asked for my usual sweet iced tea, whereas Andorra stuck with a hot green tea.

We then snagged a table near the window. "I'll see if the men can join us."

She grinned. "I like the way you think."

I called Drake since he was more critical to the case than Jaxson.

"What did Steve say?" he asked.

I told him about the list. "I thought you might like to take a look at it."

"Sure. Trace just arrived, so he can man the store, but I can't stay long. I could use something to drink, though. Jaxson and I will be there in a sec."

As soon as I disconnected, I faced Andorra. I don't know when I'd changed my mind about her, but the more I got to know her, the more I liked her. "I am really excited you're here."

"As am I. I'm just hoping my cousin and I can make a go of it as shop owners."

"Bertha is retiring for sure?" Not that Elizabeth hadn't steered me right with the last potion, but I trusted Bertha more.

"No, but she wants to cut down on her hours."

"Good to know. Before we begin, I should give you a rundown on who is in the know around here."

She laughed. "You mean Pearl, Maude, Miriam, your aunt, and Dolly?"

I was dumbfounded. "You've been here a few days and yet you know all of that?"

"Memaw is a font of knowledge. Actually, before I arrived, she gave me the lowdown."

"I'm glad she's on top of things." It made us working together easier.

Just as I pulled up the list of people at the party, Jaxson and Drake entered the tea shop. They smiled and headed over to us.

"Ladies." Jaxson leaned over and kissed me. Drake cleared his throat and motioned he was going to order. Jaxson followed him to the counter.

"Glinda, I'm so happy for you. You have a great guy," she said.

"Jaxson is wonderful. He's also a whiz on the computer."

"That makes him doubly wonderful." She grinned.

We laughed over that. As soon as the men returned, I showed them the images on my phone. "Here is the list of who was at the party. Jaxson, I know you don't know anyone, but I'm hoping you'll be able to help us sort through the names."

"I can do that, though I'm sure you'll want to enter the list into a spreadsheet first and then rank each person as to their likelihood of being the killer."

I would have laughed at that statement, except it was true. Organizing data was what I did. "Nothing is wrong with that approach."

I placed the phone where we all could see. In silence, we read the first page.

"Ronnie Taggert was there?" Drake asked. "Flying in from California is quite a big deal for a one-night get together."

"Does he have family here?" I asked.

Drake shrugged.

"I can do a little search," Jaxson offered. He pulled out his phone and typed in the name.

"You really think losing a debate tournament ten years ago would upset him that much?" I asked.

"I don't think we should eliminate anyone who has any reason not to like Kyle," Drake said.

"Works for me. Once we have a tentative list, maybe Elizabeth can help us with who might be a witch or a warlock and who isn't. Not that I thought she can tell, but she might remember who'd been in her store of late." Andorra's cousin might not know who were Witch's Cove High School graduates, but if she remembered someone in their late twenties buying those particular herbs, it would help.

Andorra nodded. "That's a good plan."

Once Maude delivered our drinks, we changed the subject and talked about what we'd been doing for the last ten years. We all seemed to understand that we didn't need anyone overhearing our conversation about murder—especially Maude.

When we finished, Andorra and I told the men we were going to check in with Elizabeth.

"If she didn't go to high school here, will she know these people?" Jaxson asked.

"Andorra knows the ingredients of the potion, and we're hoping Elizabeth will remember who she sold those items to."

"Aren't the names in the computer?" Jaxson asked.

Andorra looked to the side. "I'm afraid my grandmother wasn't big into that kind of thing."

That was a shame. I inhaled. "Let's see how good Elizabeth's memory is."

We said our goodbyes and then walked down the street to

the Hex and Bones Apothecary. The air was a little chilly, but since the sun was out, the trip was enjoyable.

The shop had a fair number of people inside. Since Elizabeth was busy with a customer, Andorra and I decided to look at some of the books of spells to see if we could find one that used the particular ingredients.

"If all of these books were electronic, it would be easier," I said. "We could do a word search."

Andorra chuckled. "Since the books look really old, I don't think anyone thought of it back then."

"It's never too late."

She laughed. "I hope you aren't suggesting I enter all of this information into a computer?"

"No one has that kind of time. It would take an army of workers to scan every page. It was wishful thinking."

If our search didn't pan out, I would introduce her to Levy. His clan excelled at finding needles in haystacks.

As soon as Elizabeth finished with her customer, she headed over to us and hugged Andorra. "Are you here to give working a try?"

"Not today, but I will soon. I promise. Do you remember me mentioning a Kyle Covington who died at the reunion?"

"Of course. It was a terrible tragedy. Did you learn if he was murdered or not?"

"We did. In fact, Glinda and I were able to help the medical examiner figure out that a spell did him in."

Elizabeth's eyes widened. "Did you touch the body?"

I was glad the cousins were open about their talents.

"I did, but only after Glinda performed a little magic of her own."

Elizabeth smiled. "I'm not surprised. What did you do?"

I explained what my necklace could detect. "It's great that it found both poison and magic, but Andorra was able to narrow down the ingredients used in the spell."

"She is talented. What can I do to help?"

Andorra nodded toward my phone. I pulled up the names of the party goers. "This is the list of reunion attendees. It's possible that one of these people did the spell on Kyle," I said.

"We were wondering if you remember if anyone who came in bought crenolen root? The sage and turmeric they could buy in any grocery store," Andorra said.

"I remember ringing up that ingredient about three days ago, but I couldn't say who bought it. I don't know many people in town yet."

"Do you recall if it was a man or a woman?" I asked.

"I don't. I'm sorry."

"Do most people pay in cash?" I asked.

"I'd say about one-third do, especially if it's not for much."

That was what I was afraid of. Cash was untraceable. I turned to Andorra. "When we narrow down our list of suspects, maybe we can get a current picture of everyone and show their image to Elizabeth. That might trigger her memory."

"Sounds great." She turned to her cousin. "I'll email you the ingredient list. Not that I'm expecting a second murder, but if anyone asks for a combination of these herbs, can you let me know?"

"Absolutely." Elizabeth glanced at me and then looked back at Andorra. "Ah, someone showed up this afternoon, and *he's* in the back room."

The tension in Elizabeth's face almost scared me. She'd keep a visitor where they stored their inventory?

"Hugo is here?" Andorra bit down on her lip.

I had to ask. "Who is Hugo?"

She faced me and grabbed my hand. "If I show you, you need to keep quiet about it. You can tell Jaxson and Rihanna, but that's all."

Now she was making me uncomfortable. "O-kay. I think."

Andorra led me to the back room. Sitting in a chair was a man about our age. His features were chiseled and his eyes rather distant.

"Hugo, we have company."

He stood and faced me. I waited for him to say something, but he didn't. "Hi, I'm Glinda."

When he didn't respond, I looked at Andorra.

"We need to talk," she said. "Hugo is mute. We communicate telepathically, because...well, he's not even human. He is only taking a human form right now."

I didn't know whether to laugh or run. "I don't understand."

She inhaled. "I'm not sure I do either. Let me start at the beginning." There were two card table chairs in the corner that she unfolded and motioned that I sit down.

Hugo didn't move. "Is he dangerous?" I whispered.

"Not to good people."

I sure hoped I was considered one of those. "And he just showed up here? You didn't know he was coming?"

Her smile came out brief. "It's a long story. The fact

Hugo is here at all implies danger lurks." She looked over at him. When Hugo shook his head, I had to surmise that she'd asked him if he knew who the killer was.

"Does he know who killed Kyle?"

Her eyes widened. I didn't think my question required a big jump.

"No, he doesn't. Hugo says evil showed up at the shop a few days ago, but he wasn't in his human form at the time, so he couldn't see the person."

I glanced at the man once more. When he remained totally still, I figured it was safe. "Go on."

"When you turned twelve, you probably went into the Hendrian Forest to do the spell for your familiar."

"Sure." I had to chuckle. "But you met Iggy. He was supposed to be a black cat, not a pink iguana."

"He's adorable, nonetheless."

"He is." I loved my familiar and don't know what life would be like without him.

"I, too, went into the forest and did the spell. I might have been young, but I was rather talented. It should have worked."

"Instead, Hugo came out from behind a tree?"

She shook her head. "No. Nothing happened. Totally devastated, I returned to the parking lot where Mom was unable to console me. Eventually, she drove me home. The whole time she kept saying that not all witches are lucky enough to have a familiar. Trust me, I didn't find a lot of comfort in that."

"Then how did you get Hugo?" Assuming he came from a spell.

"It was the next day when I was at church."

If the man hadn't been still standing in the corner, I would have thought she was pulling my leg. "You think he was sent from above?"

Chapter Five

ANDORRA LOOKED OVER at Hugo. Even though they didn't speak, I could tell she was communicating with him again, in part, because he sat down.

"Hugo was not *sent from above*, as you put it," Andorra said. "After the Sunday service, I was standing outside of the church looking up when I saw only one gargoyle on top of the roof. I thought maybe the statue had fallen off."

"Are you saying that Hugo was a gargoyle?"

She nodded. "I didn't know what happened at first. All I saw was a twelve-year-old boy standing in front of me. I could hear him in my head, but his lips weren't moving. I looked around for his parents, but no one was there. He told me not to tell my mom about him right away. And then he walked to the back of the church. I was too young to realize that he was my familiar."

I tried to put myself in that situation but couldn't. Only then did the name make sense. "Did you name him Hugo because Victor Hugo wrote *The Hunchback of Notre Dame*, and there are gargoyles everywhere in Paris?"

"Actually, Hugo told me that was his name."

All of this was a bit overwhelming. "You said he was twelve when you met him? He doesn't look that now."

"No, he ages, but he's not like other people. He doesn't eat or sleep. Hugo returns to his statue form when need be."

I'd been in the Hex and Bones Apothecary dozens of times. There had been a gargoyle near the cash register, but I assumed it was a decorative item. "When you are not here, does he remain in the store?"

"Yes. Hugo takes his human-looking form only when he needs to keep me safe."

I wasn't sure how to react. "Now that you're hopefully going to be living in Witch's Cove, will he stay at the shop at night or go home with you?"

"He stays here. His powers come from the store, which was why I couldn't take him with me to college or to New York. It was one of the reasons why I wanted to return."

"Why the store and not your house?"

"I asked Memaw about that. She thought it was because Hugo needed to be surrounded by the occult items in order to draw his energy."

"I guess that makes sense." This was a lot to digest. "Have you told Drake?"

"No, but I will. I'm not trying to hide Hugo. It's just that people may not understand him. I need to make sure they won't try to destroy him or think that I'm nuts."

"I get it. I talk to a pink iguana. Most people don't believe me when I say he can talk back. Did Hugo show himself because Kyle's killer is still in town? Does he think you might be next?"

"I think Hugo sensed the evil in town and wanted to warn me. He didn't say anything about me personally being in danger."

I looked over at the man and smiled. I thought it best to show him I was a friend and not a foe. If he could change from a stone statue to a human, no telling what else he could do.

Feeling a little uncomfortable with her familiar's constant staring, I planted my palms on my knees. "I think I'll be getting back."

Andorra stood. "I wanted to thank you for welcoming me back to Witch's Cove. It means the world to me."

I think Drake was the one who was the most welcoming, but now that I had found her, I liked her, too. "You're welcome. I take it this means you're going to stay?"

"I think so."

"I hope you do."

Before it became too awkward, I left, but not before glancing at the cash register. No gargoyle was there. Creepy. The whole idea of Hugo blew my mind, and I hoped she wasn't spinning some yarn to see how gullible I might be. For all I know, she'd hired some guy to scare me but not before moving the stone sculpture.

I was aware of quite a lot of magic, and I even had seen men change into wolves, but statues changing into humans and back again was a bit unrealistic even for my vivid imagination. Without being specific, I might have to ask Levy about the possibility of something like Hugo existing.

I figured that Drake would be at his shop, and more than likely, Jaxson would have returned to our office, so that was where I went. I really wanted to hear his take on Hugo—assuming I could convince him I wasn't making it up.

Instead of Jaxson, I found Rihanna and Casi at the office.

They were in the living room sipping a soda and eating popcorn. That was Rihanna's comfort food. "Hey, ladies."

Only after taking a careful look at Casi did I see she was upset. "What's wrong?"

"My brother is a jerk." Her lower lip trembled.

"Christian?" I had no idea how many siblings she had.

"Yes."

"What did he do?"

"When we got home last night, he basically told me to stop whining because I didn't even know Kyle. He was angry that I was sad a man had died."

That was harsh. Casi was just a kid. "You were being sympathetic or rather empathetic. I would have worried if you had been unaffected."

"That's what I told her," Rihanna said.

Casi sniffled. "My mom told me that Christian wasn't always so angry. You knew him back then. What was he like in high school?"

Because of the eight-year age gap, Casi might not remember what he was like as a teenager. I sat down on the sofa. To my surprise, Iggy crawled up next to me and didn't demand any attention for a change. "Christian and I didn't hang out, but I remember he excelled in math, because I did too."

"My brother?"

"Yes. I didn't take Economics with him, but I believe he won the year-end award for best business student. He'd written some paper on the future of fiat money—or rather its downfall." I have no idea how or why I remembered that.

Her eyes widened. "We're talking about my brother? The one who is the garage mechanic?"

"I'd heard he worked at one. I never did understand why he didn't pursue a career in business. He was accepted to the University of South Florida, if I recall, but once I left for school, I really didn't keep tabs on him or many of my classmates."

"He went to USF, but he dropped out his junior year."

"Why?" People as smart as Christian usually finished.

"He wouldn't say."

Even though Casi probably didn't know anything, I had to ask if her brother said anything to indicate he didn't like Kyle. "I can see why Christian wouldn't understand why you'd be upset over a classmate's death since you didn't know him, but was your brother sad?"

"He didn't act like it."

Interesting. "I'm sorry he was so insensitive."

Casi stood. "I need to be heading back." She hugged Rihanna and left without explaining her need for a quick departure. I had the sense I'd asked some questions that were too personal.

No sooner had Rihanna returned to her bedroom after her friend left than Jaxson came in. "Hey," I said. "What have you been up to?"

"Running around with Drake."

"Learn anything?"

"We met up with Kim Lucas, who works at the Cove Eye Clinic."

"I know Kim. Why did you need to see her?"

"Let me grab something to drink and then I'll tell you." It took him but a moment to snag a drink and return. "Kim was in charge of inviting the alums to the reunion and making the party a success."

"I bet she never expected someone would die."

"I'm sure not."

"While Kim will know who accepted the invite, we already have the list of who was there," I said.

"Agreed, but she has the alum's mailing address, their email address, phone number, or all three."

I could see the benefit of that. "Will she share?"

"If we ask for a specific name, she most definitely will."

Rihanna came in from her bedroom. "Hey, Jaxson."

"Hey, kiddo. Why so glum?" he asked.

She told him about Casi, and then I added my two cents.

"The man sounds like a jerk. Glinda, you mentioned Casi was a witch. Does that mean Christian is a warlock?"

"That's usually the way it works, but unless both parents have power, we can never be sure." I looked over at Rihanna to see if she'd disagree, but she said nothing.

"I'll do a background check on him. He and Kyle might have more in common than we know."

"Kim Lucas might remember the details of their falling out." I turned to Rihanna. "Is Mr. Strauss still at Witch's Cove High?"

"Yes."

I faced Jackson again. "Mr. Strauss teaches Economics."

Jaxson grunted. "Trust me. I remember him. He did not like me."

That might have been because Jaxson was a troublemaker back then. "I'm hoping Mr. Strauss might remember what happened between Christian and Kyle. I believe they were working together on some year-end project. I recall there had been a rift between them, but I don't recall what caused it."

"Are you thinking Christian did all the work, and Kyle got the glory?"

I chuckled. I bet Jaxson pulled that stunt a few times in high school. "Maybe."

"I'll see what I can find out." Jaxson pulled out his phone and made a note. "Drake might remember since he was Kyle's friend."

"While you're at it, maybe look in the gym for any security cameras."

"Can do," he said.

"Rihanna, do you know who made the punch for the party?"

"Casi and Lena did."

I sagged. No way did I believe either of them had anything to do with putting a spell on it. Casi might have had the ability, but she'd have no desire to harm Kyle.

"Someone had to have seen someone add some herbs to the punchbowl."

"Wouldn't they have been kind of floating on the surface?" Jaxson asked.

"Yes, unless a spell was used to dissolve them instantly. Step one is to find that spell." I pulled out my phone and made a note to ask Andorra to check with Elizabeth about it. "I will also ask Gertrude. While her specialty was more that of a psychic, she might suggest what I need to do or where to look."

"Sounds good," Jaxson said.

"There is something else I need to tell you, but this has to be kept between the three of us. Andorra will let Drake know when the time is right."

"Sure," Rihanna said.

"That includes Casi, Lena, and Gavin."

Iggy hopped up on the sofa next to me. "What about me?"

Since he couldn't tell anyone, I figured he was safe. "You can know, but don't tell Aimee."

"This must be juicy."

"I wouldn't call it juicy as much as really strange. I'd love to ask Gertrude or Levy about it, but until Andorra gives me the okay, I can't say a word."

Jaxson clasped my hand. "What is it? You sound worried."

"More confused than anything. Andorra has a familiar that is a mute gargoyle who can turn into a human-looking entity."

All three of them looked at me as if I was crazy. "How is that possible?" Rihanna asked.

I went through the whole story about how Andorra tried to do a spell for a familiar but kind of failed. "At the next church service, he appeared by her side. He only shows up when he senses danger."

"He senses danger now, I take it?" Jaxson asked.

"Yes."

"You've seen him?" Rihanna's eyes were wide as saucers.

"Yes. Mind you, I haven't communicated with him because only Andorra can."

"Does his presence convince you that Kyle's killer is close at hand?" Jaxson asked.

"To be honest, I am still trying to figure out what Hugo

is. However, Andorra seems to think danger is lurking."

"Then we need to proceed with caution," he said.

My phone rang. "Speak of the devil. It's Andorra." I'd just left her, so I was curious why she'd be calling. "Hey."

"You won't believe who just stopped into the store."

Why did people love to play guessing games with me? I didn't like them. "Who?"

"Patricia Haltern."

Several thoughts ran through my mind at once, but I'd let Andorra tell me more first. "What did she want?"

"Just to chat a bit. Her husband was dead set against her coming to the reunion, and now he's insisting they return home even though the sheriff said they have to stay in town until Kyle's death gets all sorted out. She's scared, Glinda."

Bullies were the worst. "Did she say why he didn't want her to come to the reunion?"

"No, but I have a suspicion that it had something to do with Kyle."

My pulse tripped. "Do we have any idea if her husband is a warlock?"

"I don't know. If I could run into them, I could shake his hand to see if there is any residue of the ingredients inside him, but hand shaking is the least effective method."

"Do you believe Patricia is telling the truth?" It seemed a bit odd that a friend from ten years ago would spill her heart out, but maybe she and Andorra were closer than I realized.

"Why wouldn't she be?"

I was probably jaded. "She saw you asking questions. Maybe she wants to learn what you know. It is possible Harry made her speak with you."

"Hmm. I guess that could be the case."

"What about Hugo? Can he tell you anything?" I asked.

"Hugo was in the back room at the time."

What good was he then? "Did Elizabeth recognize Patricia as the person who bought any of the potion ingredients? I mean, if Harry was the one who killed Kyle, he might have asked her to buy them for him. He could have told her he had a cold and those herbs would help."

Andorra grunted. "I can see why you're a sleuth. You have a devious mind, Glinda Goodall."

I didn't know if she meant it as a good or bad thing. "Thank you, I think."

"I meant it as a compliment. Let me noodle my interaction some more, and I'll call you later."

"Okay."

Once I disconnected, I told Rihanna and Jaxson what she'd said, though Rihanna probably could read my mind for much of it.

Jaxson pulled out his phone again. "I'll add this Harry Haltern to my growing list of suspects."

"And so, it begins," I said.

Chapter Six

JUST AS I was trying to figure out our next move, someone knocked on our office door. A second later, Steve stepped in with another man right behind him.

"I hope I'm not intruding," the sheriff said.

Jaxson and I stood. "No. Come in."

"This is Jude Walton, Kyle's business partner. He just flew in from California."

If he'd just arrived, he had nothing to do with Kyle's death. Being the murdered man's partner, though, he might be able to help us figure out why someone wanted Kyle dead. "I'm sorry for your loss."

Jude nodded. "Thanks."

After introducing him to Jaxson and Rihanna, I motioned they both take a seat. To be honest, I wasn't sure why Steve brought him to our office. Was it because he considered Jaxson and me on the case—not officially, of course, but still involved? Steve must be convinced magic was used in Kyle's death, or he wouldn't be here.

"I thought Jude might be able to give us some background information as to who would have wanted Kyle dead." Steve held up a hand. "Following up those names is my job. What I'd like to know is whether anyone of them could have been a witch or a warlock?"

Did he think Jude knew? Or me for that matter? I'd already explained that I couldn't tell. "Happy to help. Mr. Watson, do you have any idea who might have wanted Kyle dead?"

"No."

Okay, so much for a successful meeting. "Did anyone close to Kyle have any magical abilities?" That would be useful to know.

"Not that I know about. Would they have a prominent tattoo or something to indicate they knew witchcraft?"

"That would be nice, but no." This was a bust.

Steve cleared his throat. "Glinda or Jaxson, who have you zeroed in on? Maybe you could share these names with Jude. He might recognize one of them."

That might be why Steve brought Kyle's business partner here. "Yes. What about Ronnie Taggert?"

His eyes opened. "Ronnie came here?"

Goose bumps rose on my arms. "Yes. Why?"

"Ronnie used to work with me and Kyle."

I waited for him to continue, but Jude seemed uncertain about whether to speak ill of anyone. "Did something happen between the two of them?"

"You could say that." He described a project that my math brain couldn't fully understand. It involved blockchain technology, smart contracts, and decentralized finance—all gobbledygook to me. "They had a difference of opinion about whether to make the project open or closed source. That was when Ronnie decided to leave our company and start his own firm." Jude dipped his head. "It lacked financing and a vision, so he didn't fare well."

"While yours and Kyle's did, I presume." Jaxson made it sound more like a statement than a question.

"Yes."

"If we pretend Ronnie killed Kyle, what would he gain from it?" Steve asked.

"There'd be no payoff for him, which is why I find it hard to believe Ronnie is guilty," Jude said. "Unless…"

"Unless, what?" I interjected.

"Unless Ronnie's anger festered over the last two years, and his hatred grew like a cancer. He'd have no reason other than wanting revenge for Kyle being right about the future."

"That seems like a rather thin motive," I said.

"I might agree, except something happened about a week ago. Ronnie's company was on the verge of bankruptcy, and he asked Kyle for a loan. Our cash flow had been impacted lately due to economic issues, so Kyle had to turn him down."

"Not helping a friend in need is often a good motive for murder," Steve said.

"I agree, but we believe the killer used magic to kill Kyle," I added.

Jude's eyes widened. "As far as I know, Ronnie doesn't possess that kind of talent."

"Would you know if he did?" I didn't want to be mean, but Jude had already admitted he had no idea about the occult.

"I guess not."

Jaxson pulled out his phone and listed the possible suspects. "Do any of those names ring a bell?"

"No, I'm sorry. I would talk to Francine. She might know

something."

"Who's Francine?" Jaxson jotted down the name.

Jude stilled. "Kyle's fiancée. She came to Witch's Cove with him to attend his reunion."

I looked over at Steve, who suddenly sat up straighter. "I didn't see any Francine on the list of guests."

"That's because she didn't attend the party. She told me she wasn't feeling well."

That sounded like those two were cozy.

"What's her last name?" Jaxson asked before I could question Jude further.

"Xavier."

"Is Francine aware that Kyle is dead?" Steve asked. "I didn't contact her since I didn't know about her."

"She knows now. After you called me, I contacted her. Francine had no idea he'd died. Let me tell you, it was a rough phone call."

"I can only imagine, but hadn't she been a wee bit worried when Kyle didn't return to the hotel—or wherever they were staying?" I would have been if Jaxson and I were married.

"They were staying at the Magic Wand, but Francine told me that Kyle said not to wait up for him, because he intended to go out with his friends after the reunion."

I couldn't help but wonder which friends Kyle was referring to. Drake had reminded me that Kyle didn't have many. If he contacted anyone, I bet it would have been Drake. I'd have to ask my good friend if he thought there would have been a large, rowdy gathering, or whether Kyle or Francine had lied.

"Is Francine still in town?" I asked.

He nodded.

"Glinda, I'll speak with Francine and ask her to stay for a few more days. She will probably be the most helpful person in figuring out who might have wanted to harm him." He looked over at Jude. "I tried contacting Kyle's parents but couldn't get a hold of them."

"They're on a cruise in the Mediterranean, but I sent them a message. I'm expecting a response soon."

I'm not sure I'd want to know about that kind of tragedy if I was in the middle of the ocean. "Jude, it is so nice of you to fly across country to be here."

"He's my best friend—or rather was my best friend. I had to see him. And I wanted to give Francine support."

Steve turned to me. "We just came from the morgue."

"That had to have been tough."

He nodded. We listed a few more names who might want to harm Kyle, but Jude knew none of them. After talking further about his and Kyle's roles in the company, Jude and the sheriff left. Ugh. This case wasn't progressing like most of the others we'd worked on. We had suspects, sure, but no one stood out as our number one person of interest.

"That has to be tough to learn your business partner is dead. It seems as if Kyle might have been the technical brains in the company and Jude the marketing person," Jaxson said.

"I agree, and since Jude wasn't in Witch's Cove when Kyle died, it kind of eliminates him as the killer." At the moment, I wasn't ready to think he could have hired someone to poison his business partner. I turned to Rihanna, who hadn't said a word the whole time. "Did you learn anything?"

She shook her head. "Nothing other than he was genuinely distraught."

"Good to know." I wasn't sure I wanted to know the answer to the next question, but I needed to ask. "And your take on Andorra?"

Rihanna grinned and shook her head. "She's fine."

Her joy confused me, but I let it be. My cousin wouldn't steer me wrong. "I'm glad."

"Unless you need me for something, I should get back to my homework."

"Of course. Go."

As soon as Rihanna went into her room, Jaxson scooted closer. "Do you want to grab dinner?"

"I would love nothing more. It's been a hard day. I'll see what Rihanna wants to do."

I went to her bedroom, but she was on the phone. Rihanna held up a finger before telling the person on the line to hold.

"Yes?"

"Jaxson and I are headed to dinner. Want to come?"

"I would, but Gavin just asked me."

So much for doing homework. "Have fun."

To my delight, Drake was in the living room when I returned. "Hey, there." I hugged him. "I thought you might be with Andorra."

"We're going to see each other later tonight."

"I like the sound of that. Care to join us for an early dinner? We have a few new developments in the case."

"Jaxson was just filling me in. I'd love to if I won't be a third wheel."

"Never."

After a quick debate, we decided to head on over to the Tiki Hut Grill. I hadn't spent much time with my aunt, and I felt a bit guilty for not supporting her restaurant either. Just as we were about to go inside, who should be coming out but Casi's brother, Christian. That was a surprise since I'd never seen him at the restaurant before. He stopped, his gaze bouncing between me, Jaxson, and Drake.

"Christian," I said. Even though he'd been insensitive to his sister, I didn't want to make a scene. It would serve no purpose.

He stopped inches from me. "I'd appreciate it if you don't fill my sister's head with lies."

"Lies?" What was he talking about? I'd only said he should be nicer. "What did I say?"

"You all but told her I was a loser."

"I'd never use that word. Casi must have misunderstood."

"Stay away from her, you hear?"

I really wanted to ask him, *or what?* However, I realized that wouldn't have been smart. Besides, he stalked off before I could say more. Sure, I was tempted to go after him, but it wasn't as if I could do him any harm even if I wanted to.

A month or so ago, Steve had asked me if I had the ability to zap someone with electricity—like a human stun gun. I couldn't, but oh, what I wouldn't give to have that talent right now.

As if Jaxson could read my mind, he wrapped a very possessive arm around my waist and led me inside. "Leave it be, Glinda. Clearly, the guy has issues."

"No kidding."

I was upset over the encounter, but just stepping foot into

a place that had brought me a lot of joy calmed my nerves. The high season was upon us, and I was glad to see Aunt Fern's restaurant doing so well.

"I didn't expect you three to be here tonight," my aunt said as soon as she escaped from behind the check-out counter.

That might be because reservations were not required at the Tiki Hut. "A spur of the moment decision."

She hugged me and then led us to an empty table. "Enjoy. We'll have to catch up later. It's kind of busy right now." Aunt Fern smiled and then motioned with her head toward the large table checking out.

Once we sat down, I looked across the table to Drake. "I'm happy you could join us. We haven't caught up since you and Andorra met."

He grinned. "It's like a light has entered my life."

Wow. That was intense. "She is great."

Because he said he'd see her later tonight, I figure she'd tell him about Hugo at that time. "We had a visitor today."

"Jaxson briefly mentioned this mystery guest."

Between Jaxson and me, we gave him the rundown of Kyle's business partner and surprise fiancée. I also filled him in on Patricia Haltern and her unhappy husband.

"It seems as if Jude doesn't think Ronnie Taggert is guilty," Drake said.

I looked over at Jaxson, who then answered. "Jude has no idea about witchcraft so he couldn't say if Ronnie has any powers, but Jude admitted that a slowly building rage over Ronnie's faltering company could have triggered something inside him."

"Don't forget the loan Kyle refused to give Ronnie," I

said. "If Kyle had been his lender of last resort, and Kyle wasn't able to lend Ronnie money, it's possible Ronnie would lose his company to creditors because of it."

Drake's mouth pinched. "That would be tough. It could have been what set Ronnie off—if he's guilty."

"I know."

"And Christian? What was that outburst about?" Drake asked.

"I wish I knew." I told him as much of my conversation with Casi as I could remember.

"If Christian harmed Kyle, he could be feeling guilty right now and might need to take out his anger on someone," Jaxson said. "Besides, we know Christian is a warlock. He might still harbor some anger that Kyle, in theory, stole some of his business ideas from when they were back in high school and profited from it. Think about it. Kyle ends up super rich, while Christian is still in Witch's Cove working at a local garage."

"Christian could have been successful if he'd wanted to," Drake said.

"Maybe," Jaxson said. "We don't always have total control over our destiny."

Jaxson had his share of bad luck, but he'd turned it into a positive. "What about Patricia's unhappy husband? Was he afraid his wife and Kyle would rekindle their relationship after all these years?"

Drake shook his head. "I don't see it. Kyle had moved on. It would have been a one-way street."

"Patricia's husband might not have seen it that way."

Jaxson pulled out his phone. "I'll ask Steve to check Kyle's phone logs to see if he and Patricia had any recent conversations."

"They could have used social media to communicate."

"They could have."

"I can ask Andorra to talk with Patricia about it again. She might be honest about whether she still had feelings for Kyle, even after all these years. Patricia might consider Kyle as the one who *got away*."

Jaxson smiled. "I wouldn't know about that, but sure, ask Andorra. The power of a woman's ability to connect should never be underestimated."

Just then my best female friend, Penny, who was waitressing tonight, came over. I stood and hugged her. She'd been dating our forest ranger for a few months and appeared to be so happy. "You look great," I said.

"You, too. You're absolutely glowing. It's great to see the three of you together again."

"It's been a long time." Too long.

"We must have a girls' night out," she said.

"Totally."

"I'd love to stay and chat, but as you can see, the place is hopping tonight. I forgot how busy the evening shift could get. Do you all know what you want?" she asked.

That was a silly question, especially since I'd waitressed here for three years. "A number four special."

The men ordered their meals, and once Penny left to turn in our ticket, Jaxson leaned back in his chair. "How do you want to approach Francine?"

"Approach her?" I wasn't sure what he meant.

"You'll need a cover story."

I thought for a moment and then smiled. "I have the perfect plan."

Chapter Seven

"SINCE WE NEED to find out what Kyle Covington's fiancée has to say, who better to lead the discussion than Kyle's very good high school friend, Drake Harrison?" I grinned at him.

"You want me to talk to her?"

"What's wrong with that? Don't you want to offer your condolences?"

He nodded. "Actually, it will be nice to learn what he's been up to these past few years."

"I could come with you since we both knew Kyle." I winked.

"Sure. That would be great."

"Since she is staying at the Magic Wand, I'll ask Steve which room Francine is in. The hotel is often picky about giving out that kind of information."

"Go for it," Drake said.

I called Steve and explained that Drake and I wanted to offer our condolences to Francine.

He chuckled. "You just want to see if Francine can help identify who might have wanted to harm Kyle."

I was slightly insulted that he didn't believe me, though he probably was kidding. It was in his best interest if I found out anything. "I figure she's more likely to talk to us than the law."

"I'll give you that. She's in room 117."

"Thank you, and yes, I'll let you know if she gives us any insight."

I could almost see him smile over the phone. I think I was wearing the man down—albeit slowly. I disconnected and turned to my dinner partners. "It's a go."

The three of us discussed the best way to broach the topic of the potential killer. Since Steve said he planned to ask Francine to stay around, we didn't need to pick her brain about everything the first time we spoke. However, I had to be prepared if she knew nothing. I turned to Jaxson. "Have I talked much about high school?"

"Not really. I went to Witch's Cove High, and I guess I didn't think to ask you about it. Is there something I need to know?"

I loved that he thought I was worried. "No. That's the point. Kyle might not have gone into a lot of detail about his high school days. She might not even be able to name more than a few people he graduated with."

Both brothers leaned back in their seats. "That is an excellent point. Does that mean you don't want to talk to her?" Drake asked.

"No, I do, but we need to find a way to bring up Ronnie Taggert's name and maybe even Patricia's."

"Why Patricia?" Drake asked. "Do you think Kyle would have mentioned an old flame to his fiancée?"

I shrugged. "Maybe not, but if some guy wouldn't leave me alone, I can't imagine hiding it from Jaxson."

"I'm glad, but if he shows up, I'll hunt him down like the dog he is."

I laughed. "What I'm saying is that Francine might legitimately know nothing."

"Then I'll offer my condolences, and that will be that," Drake said.

I liked his sentiment. "Okay then. If it wouldn't look funny, I'd ask Rihanna to join us."

"That would make it too easy," Jaxson said.

"Why? Because we'd know if Francine was telling the truth."

"Yup."

I lifted my chin. "Personally, I think there is nothing wrong with having something easy for a change, but Francine might be overwhelmed to have three strangers show up to her room."

"I agree, so how about we ask her to meet us in the bar for a drink instead? It might be less intimidating," Drake said.

"I like it."

After we finished our meal, I hugged Jaxson goodbye.

"Call me when you are done," he said.

"Will do."

Drake and I crossed the street to the hotel and then entered the lobby. The place was busy, but with the reunion in town, a crowd was to be expected. "Let's sit in the bar and order a drink. Then we can call her."

"Would you mind if I asked Andorra to join us?" he asked.

I can't believe I hadn't thought of that. "Actually, it might seem less intimidating for Francine. It will look like we're just a bunch of high school friends who want to remember Kyle."

He pulled out his cell and dialed Andorra's number and briefly explained our plan. "If you can join us, we'll be in the hotel bar." He nodded. "See you soon."

"She's coming?"

"Yup. She's actually at the Hex and Bones now. It will only take her a minute to get here."

"Great."

Once inside, we grabbed a booth large enough for six. If a couple of alums decided to join us, we'd have room. After we ordered a drink, Drake called Francine's room, and I was impressed with his kindness over her loss. While it took some work to convince her to have a drink with us, she finally agreed. If anything happened to a loved one of mine, I'd want to commiserate with others who knew that person.

Just as the server delivered our drinks, Andorra showed up, and Drake lit up as he watched her move toward us. She kissed him on the cheek and then smiled at me. I was so happy Drake had found a great girl.

"Where's Francine?" Andorra asked.

"She's coming," he said. "It took some convincing."

"I imagine she'll want to look her best," Andorra said.

"Why? If I'd lost someone, I'd be too distraught to care about what I looked like."

"She's from Silicon Valley."

Was that supposed to explain it? Before I could ask her, a tall, slim brunette with long, wavy hair came into the bar. There was little doubt in my mind that this was Francine Xavier. Why? She was wearing a very expensive-looking tight black suit with a white silk blouse and matching black and white four-inch spiked heels. Add in manicured nails and makeup that I could only dream of being able to achieve, and it screamed of rich elegance.

"Drake, that's got to be her," I whispered.

He stood, and then Andorra and I followed suit.

"Francine?" Drake asked as she came toward us.

Her smile was brief. "Yes."

We sat back down, and I scooted over to make room. I shook her hand and introduced myself, in part because I wanted it to look natural when Andorra touched Francine's hand. Not that I thought the woman had killed her fiancée, but it never hurt to be thorough.

Drake motioned for the waiter. "What can I get you to drink?" he asked.

"A chardonnay." She then turned to us. "Did you see him?"

Drake nodded, but I shook my head. I hadn't gone to see the body.

"He looked peaceful," Drake said.

"That's good. I still can't believe Kyle is gone. He was so vibrant." Francine swiped a finger under her eye.

"Poison can kill even the strongest." If Steve had spoken with her, she had to know how Kyle died.

She nodded. "I know, but who would have killed him?"

The sleuth in me rejoiced that she'd broached the topic. "We were kind of hoping you had an idea."

Her eyes widened. "Me? I have never met any of his friends from here, and it wasn't like he talked about his high school days very often."

Too bad. "Did you know that Ronnie Taggert came back

for the reunion?"

"Jude told me. Do you think he killed Kyle?"

My heart skipped a beat. Why would she suggest that? "I couldn't say."

"I personally don't see it," Drake said. "Kyle, Ronnie, and I used to debate together. All three of us had a friendly rivalry, but that was all."

"I'd heard about that. It was why Ronnie came to work with Kyle. They were friends," she said.

"Jude said they had a falling out," Drake said.

Francine nodded. "A difference of opinion. About five years ago, Kyle and Ronnie, who were programmers, formed the Digital Income Investment Group with Jude. Two years later, they had a big difference of opinion about whether to share their software with the world."

That matched what Jude had said. "If he is guilty, why would he take so long to exact his revenge?"

"Recently, Ronnie's company started losing money big time. Kyle invested in some digital currencies that did well, whereas Ronnie chose riskier investments. All I know is that Ronnie came to Kyle maybe a week ago asking for a loan."

I wanted to see if her story matched Jude's. "Did Kyle lend him the money?"

"No. He thought it was a bad use of funds."

"Could the Digital Income Investment Group have funded it?"

"Of course."

Someone was lying then. Maybe Kyle didn't want his fiancée to know his company was going through a rough patch. I could understand keeping that a secret—at least for a while.

"What does Jude make of all of this?" Andorra asked.

"He has no idea if Ronnie is involved or not. Nor does he know who else would have wanted to harm Kyle," Francine said.

"What about Patricia Haltern's husband?" Andorra asked.

"Who?"

"Patricia Haltern used to be Patricia Diaz. She and Kyle dated in high school."

Francine huffed out a laugh. "You think a former girlfriend would harm Kyle?"

"No, but her very possessive husband might," I tossed in.

Francine sipped her drink. If only Rihanna were here, I'd know what the woman was thinking. Grief, of course, but it seemed like more than that. Only what? Outrage or a need for revenge maybe?

"I didn't know anything about this former girlfriend or her possessive husband. I'm betting Kyle didn't mention her, because they hadn't been in contact for the last ten years. Kind of like the old saying, out of sight, out of mind."

That made sense. To be honest, I loved Jaxson, yet there were a lot of things about his past I didn't know either. Quite frankly, I didn't want to know since high school hadn't been a particularly good point in his life. Besides, he'd changed since then.

"Did Kyle ever tell you about his last high school debate that he won?" Drake said.

"No." A small smile lifted her lips.

Bless his heart for steering the conversation away from Kyle's death and more toward the good times in his life. I only had a few stories to add, but I was happy to talk about them. He'd always been nice to me, even when I beat him on a math test.

For the next hour, it was mostly Drake who told stories about his friend. I couldn't help but feel sorry for his loss. Drake really had fond memories of their friendship. It was equally sad that they'd lost touch.

After Francine finished her second drink, I could see her fatigue.

"I need to head to bed. It's been a long day," she said.

"I can only imagine."

She thanked us again for helping to bring Kyle to life and then went to her room.

I spun toward Andorra. "Well?"

She sucked in a breath. "I might have sensed something when I shook her hand, but if she'd used sage for something else, it would be in her system. I can't say for sure that she had all of the ingredients in her."

"Maybe she used gloves."

"A smart witch would."

Yikes, I would never think of doing that. Until I'd met Andorra, I wasn't even aware anyone could tell what herbs a person had touched.

I turned to Drake. "Your take?"

"I'm not sure. When I told her some stories about Kyle's debate victories, and a few of his wrestling successes, I felt as if I was talking to a wall."

"Ouch. Are you saying she wasn't grieving?"

He shrugged. "I don't know what I'm saying. I guess I knew the old Kyle, and she fell in love with the wealthy entrepreneur. They barely seem like the same person."

Andorra polished off her drink. "She does seem to have embraced the rich life style, though she might come from money. I met many like her in New York City."

I wasn't sure what that implied, but it didn't sound good. "Is there anything we can tell Steve about our discussion?"

Andorra and Drake looked at each other. I know she could use mental telepathy with Hugo, her gargoyle familiar, but it was almost as if she and Drake were communicating that way now.

"Not really. She didn't suggest anyone who might have wanted Kyle dead, which makes sense since Francine didn't seem to know much about the Kyle of old," he said.

I mentioned the discrepancy between Jude's account of the loan request and Francine's.

"Kyle might not have confided in her about his financial state," Drake said.

"I thought that might be the case." I held up my glass. "At least we tried. Should we scratch Jude Watson off the list since he was still in California at the time of Kyle's demise?"

"Yes, unless he hired someone to poison his partner," Drake said.

"Why would he? What would he gain from Kyle's death? There has to be a motive," Andorra added.

"Do we know the terms of the partnership, like if Jude gets full ownership of the company if Kyle dies?" I looked over at Andorra, but she shrugged. "Steve might be able to find out."

"Could Francine maybe receive something?" Andorra said. "I know they weren't married yet, but he could have left her his home or his bank account. We should have asked what she did for a living."

"Assuming she worked. There are women who think that if they marry a rich guy that they won't have to work ever again."

"If that were the case here, she would have waited until after they wed to do him in," Drake said."

"True. Personally, I would be totally bored sitting around all day," I said.

"Me, too," Andorra said.

Drake leaned back in the booth. "Not me. If some woman wants to support me, I won't turn it down." He flashed Andorra a grin.

I threw my napkin at him. "You couldn't last a week. I've never known anyone who works harder than you."

"I'd like to give it a go."

We all laughed, something that I suspected we all sorely needed.

Chapter Eight

THE NEXT MORNING, I was ready to tackle this case head
on. Most of the items on the to-do list, though, required
Jaxson to investigate. I had texted him a few things last night
when I returned home from the bar at the Magic Wand hotel.
No surprise, Jaxson immediately texted me back saying he was
on it. I knew better than to bug him about things, but I
couldn't help myself. I was a bit of a control freak.

When Iggy and I entered our office, Jaxson was at his
desk. He looked up at me and smiled. "Hey. You'll be happy
to know I've been busy."

I loved it when he was industrious. I lifted Iggy out of my
purse and placed him on the floor. He immediately went over
to the heating pad. Poor guy. Winter lasted longer than usual
this year. Thank goodness, it would be spring soon.

"What did you find out?" I pulled up a chair next to him.

"I started looking into Ronnie Taggert. He was a member
of the Digital Income Investment Group for a few years and
then started his own company. As to why he came back here?
His sister, who now lives in Summertime, just delivered a
baby."

"Oh, wow. Ronnie's appearance in Witch's Cove might
have nothing to do with Kyle and everything to do with his

new nephew or niece."

"Yes, but that doesn't eliminate him as a suspect. He had a reason for being angry at Kyle if his loan was denied."

"Were you able to get any details on his company's financials?"

"No. Unless Steve has proof Ronnie might have killed Kyle, I doubt he can subpoena a California bank either, but I'm no lawyer."

"Great try, though. Did you learn anything else?"

Jaxson nodded. "I contacted Steve and asked if he planned to look into Kyle's phone logs."

"I imagine Steve would have requested permission, but do you think he knows what to look for?"

Jaxson wagged a finger. "Yes and no. Steve hopes to get access, but he admitted he didn't have a specific goal. I explained that Kyle and Patricia might have had some interactions, which meant Harry, the husband could have seen these messages and worried his wife would want to get back with Kyle."

"I like the theory, but I'm not sure I would use a phone for my interactions. They're too easy to trace."

Jaxson's brows rose. "Should I be worried?"

I grinned and then punched him in the arm. "No, silly, but as I mentioned before, they might have used some social media messaging system which would be harder to get access to—court order or not."

He shrugged. "Let's see what Steve comes up with first."

"And the gym cameras? Did they have surveillance?"

He looked at his watch. "How long do you think I've been at work?"

I was being pushy again. "Sorry."

"No problem. Actually, I have an appointment with Mr. Strauss, the Economics teacher, this afternoon to see if he remembers if Kyle and Christian Durango had a beef with each other. While I am there, I'll see about the surveillance cameras."

"I am officially impressed."

He grinned. "I aim to please. What are your plans for the rest of the day?"

"You seem to have taken care of almost all of the loose ends." I snapped my fingers. "What would be great would be if we could get some photos of Patricia's husband, Harry, as well as Ronnie and Christian to show Elizabeth. Someone has to have purchased the ingredients for the spell."

"Why not look on social media?"

"I can try, but too often people don't use pictures of themselves, but rather their kids or animals. If you look at my page, I use a picture of Iggy."

"I remember that. If you can't find any photos, I can ask Steve to access their driver's license photo. Better yet, we can use their images from the camera footage."

"That might be best. Have Drake help you pick out who is who if I'm not here."

"I'll see what I can do, but no promises. In either case, I think I should ask for a raise."

I laughed. "I had no idea we were being paid to do this."

"Hmm. That is a problem. You never said what your plans are. Get your nails done, have tea with Andorra, or chat with Penny and your other friends?"

My mouth dropped open. "No, I plan to work on this

case. For starters, I want to consult with Jude about what Francine told us to make sure she didn't lie."

"Are you saying you didn't believe her? She wasn't even at the party."

"Just covering all my bases. And after I speak with Jude, I'll probably touch base with Andorra and Drake."

"I thought you needed to speak with Gertrude about what kind of spell could have killed Kyle?" Jaxson asked.

"I touched base with her already, but she suggested I talk to Bertha. Elizabeth is on it."

"Sounds like you have things under control."

"I hope so." Though I wasn't all that sure.

"If I'm not here when you return, I'll be at the school."

"Great."

Since Steve would know how to contact Jude, I headed over to the sheriff's office. The sun was out and the town was hopping with tourists. I entered the sheriff's department and walked up to Pearl's reception desk.

"Glinda, how are things going?" she asked.

That was her way of gathering intel. "Slowly. It takes time to talk to so many from my class." In reality, I'd really only spoken to a couple of people.

"It must be nice to see your old friends."

I smiled. "It is."

Sadly, I didn't have a lot of them in high school. Other than Drake, they were far and few between.

"Steve's in his office if you want to see him."

"Thank you, Pearl."

When I knocked and entered, he didn't seem the least bit surprised. "Have you figured out who the murderer is yet?"

Wasn't he in a funny mood today? "No. Andorra, Drake, and I spoke with Francine last night, though."

His brows rose. Steve pulled open his drawer, withdrew his yellow note pad, and grabbed a pencil. "What was your impression?"

"I'm not sure. She seemed a bit cold, but it could be because she'd just lost her fiancé. Did you learn anything about her background?"

He chuckled. "I thought you came here to tell me something."

"Fine. When Andorra touched Francine's hand, she thought she sensed the herb sage, one of the ingredients in Kyles' body. That hardly constitutes proof, however. I was wondering if Francine had any motive whatsoever to want Kyle dead. Do you know if he had a life insurance policy that gave her something, even though they hadn't married yet?"

"I didn't ask, and I'm not sure if I can find out even if I wanted to. It's not like I'm a sheriff in California. Besides, she's not even a suspect yet. I'd need probable cause."

That could be an obstacle. "Then I'll ask Jude. He might know."

"I take it you don't trust her?"

I shrugged. "Not completely, but I can't point to any one thing."

"Maybe because you haven't seen her wear pink?"

"Ha, ha." I told him about Ronnie's sister delivering a baby. "It could be why he returned to Florida. Andorra is friends with Patricia, so she'll tackle that end of things."

Steve crossed his arms over his chest. "I think I'm liking this. I'll get the credit for bringing the murderer to justice just as soon as you deliver him or her to me. With proof, of course."

"As always, but remember if magic was used, I don't know what you could have done. You need me." I grinned.

He dipped his chin. "Are you saying I'm obsolete in Witch's Cove?"

He was kidding, but it was nice to see him relaxed for a change. "Absolutely not. You're the only one with a gun, so I guess you have your use."

"Ouch."

"By the way, I didn't get Jude's contact information before, and I'd like to talk with him."

Steve pulled out his phone and gave me his number. "He's also staying at the Magic Wand. He's in room 119."

My spidey sense shot to high alert. "Convenient that he and Francine are next to each other."

"You'd have to ask one of the Billows brothers whether that was a coincidence or if Jude asked to be next to her?"

"The owners wouldn't tell me even if I asked nicely. They are way too tight-lipped."

"Those two men might be the only two people in Witch's Cove who can keep a secret," he mumbled.

"You might be right."

I pushed back my chair and thanked him again. Next up was speaking with Kyle's partner. I thought about seeing if Drake or Andorra wanted to join me, but I didn't want Jude to think he was being ambushed.

Since the Magic Wand Hotel was so close to the sheriff's department, I walked there. Once in the lobby, I called Jude.

"Hello?"

"Hi, this is Glinda Goodall. Sheriff Rocker introduced us at my agency."

"Ah, yes. Glinda. What can I do for you? Or do you have news for me?"

"Can we chat about Kyle?" I purposefully didn't answer his question.

"Sure. When?"

"I'm in the lobby."

"Great. Be right there."

He quickly disconnected. It sounded like he'd been watching television, because I thought I heard someone say something in the background. It was possible it was Francine. After all, they both cared for Kyle, so it made sense they'd be together, especially since they were two strangers stuck in Witch's Cove.

I didn't have time to be nervous, because moments later, Jude entered the lobby. He spotted me and came over. "Do you know something?"

I hadn't meant to mislead him. "Not yet, partly because I don't work for the sheriff's department, nor do I have access to much information. I'm more or less an unpaid consultant. I, along with some friends, know magic, which may come in handy in capturing the killer." I led him over to a quiet corner where we could talk in private.

"You're sure magic was involved in Kyle's death?"

"Yes."

"I have no such abilities, nor do I know of anyone who does."

I believed him. "Here's the thing. Witches and warlocks usually don't go around telling people that they have powers.

We don't have anything on our bodies to indicate who we are either. Kyle could have been a warlock for all we know."

He whistled. "Seriously?"

"Yes, but we may never know."

"What can I do for you?"

I appreciated that he wanted to help. "I'm trying to find out who would want Kyle dead. Without a starting point, it will be hard to get answers."

"I told you before that I don't know. Kyle didn't talk much about his past."

"I believe you that you don't know."

He sat up straighter. "What do you mean by that?"

I hadn't meant to offend him. "The sheriff is working on getting access to Kyle's phone records."

"Why?"

"Remember, I mentioned a former flame of his? A Patricia Diaz Haltern?"

"Yes."

"We want to see if the two of them communicated before he came out here."

"He never mentioned her name."

"See? That's what I mean. That was helpful."

"Oh. You think I can eliminate a suspect, maybe?"

"Yes. Here's the thing about Patricia. I know that Kyle was in love with Francine, but Patricia might not have known that. That's why I thought she might have called him."

"That makes sense, but if she did, Kyle never told me."

"He could have been embarrassed that a ten-year-old crush contacted him."

"Possibly."

I wanted to dig into Francine further. "When Francine spoke with us last night, I forgot to ask what she did for a living. It might help put the pieces in perspective." Actually, I was mostly just nosy.

"She is the accountant for our firm."

Whoa. I didn't see that coming. If she did the company's books, she'd know whether he could or couldn't afford the loan to Ronnie. That sort of implied Jude might have lied. I cleared my throat, needing a moment to come up with another topic of conversation. "Good to know. So, when were Francine and Kyle going to be married?"

He blew out a breath. "I don't know."

I stilled. "Hadn't they set a date?"

"They did, and then Kyle told Francine he wanted to wait until the business improved."

"I take it Francine wasn't thrilled with this new wrinkle?"

"No, but like all women, she thought she could change his mind. If he loved her, he should want her to share in his successes and failures."

"I see. Did she come out here thinking she could convince him?" I was proud of myself for not laughing at that line of thought.

"Hey, I stayed out of it."

Just then, Francine entered the lobby. She stopped for a moment when she spotted us. Not wanting to get between these two, I stood.

"What's going on?" Francine sounded a tad jealous, or maybe she was scared. That, or my imagination was on overdrive.

"Glinda wanted to follow up on some suspects."

Her shoulders relaxed. "Oh."

"I'll let you two do your thing," I said.

She smiled sweetly. "I just need Jude for a little while to help me finalize the funeral arrangements. We decided to have the service in Witch's Cove since I thought Kyle would have liked that."

"I think he would have." Now wasn't the time to mention that my parents ran the funeral home. I turned to Jude. "Did his parents ever get back to you?"

"In fact, they called this morning. They were able to arrange transportation here—or so they believe. Kyle's parents are determined to make it to the service."

"That's great." I was worried we'd have to change the date. "I'll see you there then."

I couldn't leave fast enough. Once outside, I practically ran across the street and up the office stairs, hoping to find Jaxson. When I stepped inside, only Iggy was there. "Did Jaxson leave already?" I hadn't been gone long.

"No, he's downstairs with Drake. I can still hear them."

"Thank you."

Without asking if my familiar wanted to come, I rushed down the back staircase and found them in the office.

"How did it go?" Jaxson asked.

"It was quite interesting." I told them about Kyle wanting to delay the wedding and how Francine came out here to change his mind. "And get this. She is the accountant for their company." I wiggled my eyebrows.

"How is that really pertinent?" Drake asked.

"Maybe she decided to kill Kyle and set her sights on Jude if her fiancé wasn't willing to tie the knot right away. I don't know."

Jaxson smiled. "I do love your imagination. Did Jude hint this might be the case?"

"No, but how about checking Francine's social media. Maybe she commented on Jude's page more than usual, or vice versa."

"Just as soon as I return from meeting with Mr. Strauss, I'll get on it." He kissed me goodbye and left.

"What are you thinking, Glinda?" Drake asked. "I can see the wheels turning."

"I'm not sure, but Francine doesn't seem like a nice person."

He huffed out a laugh. "What would be her motive for killing Kyle, if that is what you're thinking?"

"Revenge, maybe?"

"Because he didn't want to marry her right away? Killing him wouldn't achieve her goal either."

"I'm overthinking this, aren't I?"

"Just a tad."

"It's possible Francine decided to go after Jude instead. Maybe he's been holding a torch for her all these years, and she decided to take advantage of that fact."

"Here's a thought. Could she and Jude be in it together?" Drake suggested.

I sucked in a breath. "I don't see it, but with Kyle gone, Jude might be a bit richer."

Drake wagged a finger. "I wonder if our good sheriff has learned who stood to inherit Kyle's money and his portion of the company? He was an only child, but Kyle could have named his parents as his beneficiaries, unless the partnership agreement said otherwise."

"Maybe, but if Steve knows, why didn't he tell me when I stopped over?" I thought we were sharing what we'd learned.

"He can't share everything. There are laws, you know."

"That's beside the point. He should make an exception for me." I huffed out a breath. "The other day, Jude mentioned that Kyle told Francine not to wait up for him after the reunion, because he wanted to spend time with his old friends. Could you take a guess how many good friends Kyle had from high school?"

Drake whistled. "Besides me and Ronnie?"

"Sure."

He counted on his fingers. "Ah, that would be none."

"Then why tell Francine not to wait up for him?" I asked.

"Looks like someone lied." Drake tilted his head, acting as if I should have figured it out.

"It certainly does."

Chapter Nine

THE NEXT TWO days were a bust as far as getting any closer to figuring out who'd killed Kyle. My mom, however, was making progress, working hard to organize his funeral. If we didn't figure out who was guilty by then, all parties would leave town—at least all those who didn't live in Witch's Cove.

I needed to check the facts once more to make sure I wasn't overlooking something. I refused to believe we couldn't figure this out. Our usual way of handling things in the past was to do some kind of sting operation to trap the killer, but if we didn't know who to target, how could we set one up?

Jaxson's trip to the high school hadn't really panned out as I'd hoped. While Mr. Strauss remembered Kyle Covington and Christian Durango, he couldn't recall what their project had been. Considering the number of students he'd taught, it wasn't all that surprising, just disappointing.

When I entered our office, Jaxson was at the desk, looking through more social media posts. I slipped into the chair next to him. "Has the sheriff gotten back with you about the film from the gym?"

"Yes, and he said no one was near the punch when Kyle collapsed."

"One of our suspects could have been across the room. The origin of the magic doesn't need to be close to the subject in order to work."

He turned his chair around. "Are you saying you want to look at the video?"

Jaxson had a knack for interpreting what I said. "I do, but first I want to talk with Andorra. Do you want to come?"

"How about taking my brother instead?"

That was code for Jaxson needed to work. "I can ask him."

My cute little familiar waddled toward me. "I'm coming, and I won't take no for an answer."

"Is that so?"

"Yes. You've shut me out of this case, and I resent it."

I laughed. "I've hardly shut you out. In fact, we haven't done much, so you haven't missed any of the action. Hop in my bag then."

"I'll need a sweater."

He was a very needy animal, but considering he was cold-blooded, I understood. I dressed Iggy and then called Andorra.

"Hey, Glinda."

"Do you have a minute to discuss this case? I am so frustrated."

"Sure, but you'll have to come to the store. Elizabeth is running some errands and put me in charge."

"No problem. Mind if Drake tags along, assuming he can get away?"

She chuckled. "What do you think?"

I loved how happy she seemed. "See you in a bit."

After I explained to Drake that I wanted to give this suspect list one more look, he agreed to come with me. I wasn't so naïve to think he was there only to help solve the mystery of Kyle's death.

The Hex and Bones shop was mostly empty, though a young clerk was helping a customer over in the candle section.

Andorra waved to us from the counter. "Sorry, we had to meet here," she said.

"No, it's fine."

"Mind if we sit in the back? We don't know what ears might be around."

I hadn't considered that one of our suspects might ask someone to spy on us. "Sure." I turned to Drake. "Have you met Hugo?"

"I have, but he kind of creeps me out."

I chuckled. "Me, too."

"He's harmless," Andorra said. "At least he is to those who are my friends."

Or so she thinks. We entered the back room where Andorra had a portable white board set up. "Can we use that?" I know I sounded way too excited, but that was the teacher in me reacting.

"That's why I dragged it out here."

Mentally donning my professor's hat, I walked up to the board, picked up the marker, and drew four vertical lines. "As far as I can tell, we have four suspects: Christian Durango, Francine Xavier, Patricia's husband, Harry Haltern, and Ronnie Taggert."

"What about Patricia, herself?" Drake asked.

That was a stretch. I turned to Andorra. "Did you speak

with her again to find out if she'd contacted Kyle?"

"I asked her, but she swears she didn't. She only found out from Kim Lucas that Kyle was coming a few days before the reunion."

"Did you get the sense that she wanted to pick up where she and Kyle left off?" Drake asked.

Andorra let out a long breath. "She was quite upset over his death, so maybe she came here in order to see if there was any possibility of getting back together. I don't know. Clearly, she had no idea that Kyle was engaged."

"If she was looking to be with Kyle again, that might mean she was about to leave her husband. It would be hard to have a cross-country relationship without her husband finding out," Drake said.

I looked from one to the other. "Any suggestion what number we should assign the likelihood that either Patricia or Harry killed Kyle?"

"I never spoke with Harry," Andorra said, "but I'd give him a five out of ten and Patricia a two."

I broke Harry's column into two parts and wrote down the numbers. Underneath, I listed the motive as jealousy. "Does this look good?"

"Yes," Drake said.

"Okay, what about Francine?" I gave them my take on the wedding delay that might have caused her to be so mad that she decided to set her sights on the easier going, and now possibly richer, Jude. "Or am I totally off base?"

"Sounds logical," Andorra said. "Are you discounting Jude as a possible suspect? Who's to say he's not in on it with Francine?"

"It could be, I suppose."

"Do we know for certain that he's not a little in love with her? Jude could have hired someone to kill his partner to get rid of the competition."

"You make a good point, but don't forget he said their company had a cash flow problem. It's possible he saw the only way out was to get rid of his partner." I held up a hand to indicate I wasn't finished. "And if we're making things up, Jude could have told Francine that if she killed Kyle, she could have half of Kyle's money from his half of the company."

"Wow. That is out there, Glinda," Drake said.

I looked over at Hugo. "Does he have any thoughts?"

"Hugo doesn't leave the store," Andorra said.

"I know, but maybe he sensed some evil of late," I said.

Andorra spun toward Hugo. "You did?" she asked.

Iggy popped his head out of my bag. "When was this?" he asked.

I tapped his head lightly. "Don't bother. Hugo can only communicate with Andorra."

"That's not true. I can hear him."

I stilled. Iggy didn't lie. I looked over at Andorra. "Is that possible?"

Her mouth opened and then closed. She glanced over at Hugo. "Can you explain it? Oh."

Before she could tell me, Iggy lifted his chest. "I told you I was special."

"That's good to know." I didn't see how that could help us, but I was happy Iggy might consider himself more part of the team. "What did Hugo say?"

"He felt something about an hour ago," Iggy announced.

When Andorra didn't deny it, I guess that proved Iggy and Hugo could communicate with each other. "Could he tell where the evil came from?"

Iggy climbed out of my bag and waddled over to Hugo. I held my breath, hoping the part human familiar didn't hurt him. Iggy turned around. "No, but he could tell Elizabeth was upset."

Andorra rushed over to Hugo. "Elizabeth? What was she upset about?"

I waited a beat. "What did he say?"

She shook her head. "He doesn't know. I thought something was off with my cousin. I was in the back looking for some ingredient for a customer when Elizabeth came in. She asked if I'd man the store because she had an errand to run."

"Did she say what kind of errand or when she'd be back?" Drake asked.

"No, but I wasn't really paying attention. Thankfully, Hugo had been, but I wished he'd have said something earlier."

She turned to him and seemed to listen. A two-way silent conversation was frustrating. I wondered if Iggy could read Andorra's thoughts.

"What did he say?" Now I understood how hard it was on non-magical people when I communicated with Iggy.

"Hugo was hoping he'd misunderstood the tension coming off her."

"When Elizabeth returns, I imagine she'll explain." At least I hoped that was true.

"Ladies, let's give Francine a number." Drake clearly wanted us to work on one thing at a time.

I'm glad Drake was here to keep us on track. "I'll give her an eight."

"Sounds good," Andorra added.

"Me, three," he said.

I wrote revenge as the motive. "Next is Christian." I explained that Mr. Strauss didn't recall the issue between the two boys. "The fact Christian is a warlock shouldn't condemn him. He might have been a jerk to his sister, but that could have been because he was upset over Kyle's death."

"Agreed," Drake said. "If you need a number, then a three."

Once Andorra and I agreed, I jotted it down, along with revenge for stealing Christian's business ideas. Of course, I was guessing.

"And lastly, Ronnie Taggert."

We went back and forth on his possible involvement. His sister giving birth kind of dropped him down a notch, unless he was involved with Jude for some other reason. After much debate, we decided on a six for him. He might have been angry at how Kyle treated him.

"If Francine is our top choice, what do we do about it?" We had absolutely no proof she was involved in any way. Furthermore, we had no proof she had any witch talents.

"Unless she hired someone to do her dirty work, she'd have to have been at the party," Andorra said.

"Maybe it's time we watch the video of the dance. It had only just started when Kyle was killed. It can't be too long," I said.

"You and Drake go ahead. I need to watch the store."

"Okay."

We hugged her goodbye and stepped into the main showroom. We hadn't gone more than five feet when who should come through the front door but Elizabeth. The storage room door opened, and Iggy came out.

"Were you going to leave me here?" Iggy was not pleased.

My heart almost stopped. I was so preoccupied with the case that I'd forgotten him. "Of course not. I'm sure you could have asked Andorra to call us if we had left."

"So you say."

I picked him up and placed him in my bag. "Sorry."

"That's okay. I was getting to know Hugo."

"Is he nice?"

"Yes. I like him," Iggy announced.

Andorra came out from the back and halted when she spotted her cousin. "Elizabeth, is everything okay?"

Her cousin, who was rather shy, worked her fingers together. "Yes, of course. Why wouldn't it be?"

"Hugo thought something had upset you."

She waved a hand. "I had to go to the doctors for a quick check up on something." Her brows rose as if she didn't want to talk about it in front of Drake.

"Thanks again, Andorra," I said, trying to save Elizabeth further embarrassment. "We'll let you know if the video shows anything."

"You do that." She looked over at Drake and motioned that he call her.

Drake grinned and nodded. Aw. They were too cute together.

When we arrived at the sheriff's office, Steve was out, but Nash was there so we explained our situation to him.

"Steve told me he'd watched the video, but since he didn't know any of the players, he mentioned he was going to ask you two to give it a go. Are you up for it?"

"Sure," we answered in unison.

"Then come with me."

Pride filled me as Nash led us into the conference room where he set up the video on a large screen. I loved it that Steve valued our opinion.

"I'll let you two do your thing."

Once Nash left, we turned it on. "Oh, look, there's Marty Holder. I haven't seen him in years," I said.

"Did you know he became a doctor?" Drake asked.

"I had no idea. Good for him."

For the next few minutes, I carefully watched each person who entered the gym. Unfortunately, many kept their back to the camera the whole time.

"There is Casi putting the punch on the table, so if someone put those spices in there, it would have to have been done earlier," I said.

"True. Here comes a caterer with a tray of cookies." Drake pointed to the woman who had short blonde hair, was rather tall, and quite thin.

She, too, kept her face averted to the camera. I wouldn't have thought anything about it until she'd set down the tray. It was then that I saw it. "Replay that last part."

He did. "What did you see?"

I leaned back in the seat. "Gotcha."

Chapter Ten

"**W**HAT IS IT?" Drake asked.

I pointed to the woman's nail polish. "See that artwork?"

Drake squinted and leaned forward. "It looks like a D with the letter G overlapping it a bit and positioned a little below it. I can't believe the camera was able to pick that up. It came from the one above the gym door, which is close to the table."

I pulled up the Internet on my phone and typed in the Digital Income Investment Group logo. I held it up to him. "Look familiar?"

He glanced between my phone and the video. "It's the same design. Is that…?"

"Francine? Yup. Francine in a wig." I took a picture of the image, trying to zoom in on the logo. Because it was on one of her nails, it was rather small.

He pressed the play button. "Let's see if we can see her face. The woman is keeping her head down the whole time. It's as if she knows where the cameras are located. If so, she should have worn gloves to cover her nail art. We should ask Steve to look in Francine's room for a blonde wig," he said.

"I wish we had taken pictures of her the night we were at

the bar. Then we might have an image of her wearing that nail art."

He pushed back his chair. "Let's tell Nash. If nothing else, he can question her about it. I would think he'd need to get a court order to search for the blonde wig though. Francine wouldn't turn that over willingly. Though if she's smart, she will have ditched it."

"True."

We found Nash. "Find anything?" he asked.

"Yes." I explained about the fact that Francine claimed she wasn't at the reunion yet she was dressed as a caterer.

"Are you sure? I would imagine Kyle would have recognized her."

"She had on a blonde wig and left before Kyle arrived, or should I say, she kept out of the camera view by the time he arrived."

He nodded. "That sounds suspicious. I'll find out who catered the event and then speak with Francine."

"I'll forward you the image of her nail in case she tells you you're lying." I pressed a few buttons and sent him the image.

"Thank you."

"Good luck."

Even though I was now fairly certain Francine was behind Kyle's death, we had a long way to go before we could prove she was guilty. If confronted, she might say that she was there to spy on him, claiming Kyle had to have a reason for why he suddenly decided they needed to delay their wedding. She might claim there was another woman. And to think I'd provided her with Patricia Diaz Haltern's name. Shame on me.

As soon as I returned to our office, Drake headed back to his store, and I told Jaxson all about our findings.

"That's fantastic, but you know my next question," Jaxson said.

"Yes, I do. How do we prove Francine poisoned the punch? Just because an alum's fiancée was helping out at the party, it doesn't prove she's a killer."

"Exactly. Did you see her tamper with the punch bowl?" Jaxson was an expert at shooting holes in my theory.

"No," I admitted.

"Hopefully, she'll have a good reason for why she was there."

"Francine claimed not to have heard of Patricia until after Kyle was dead," I said. "If she says she was there to spy on him because she wanted to make sure Kyle wasn't interested in rekindling the relationship with his high school sweetheart, it will prove she knew about Patricia before I'd mentioned her."

"You're right. For now, let's forget her stated reason for sneaking about. You said a sorcerer didn't need to get close to the punch bowl in order to put a spell on it?"

"She doesn't."

He crossed his arms over his chest. "If a witch did poison the punch, why didn't others get sick from it?"

I thought we'd been through this. "She probably added the ingredients to the soda bottles before the dance started and then said a spell to dissolve the ingredients. When Kyle poured his glass, she said a separate spell directed at his cup, which activated them. I will be honest. I've never met a witch with that kind of pinpoint accuracy, but I can't say it's impossible."

"Is it possible the second spell poisoned the whole bowl, but since Kyle knocked it over, no one had the chance to drink from it?" he asked.

"It's a definite possibility. Steve said he was having the punch tested. We should also ask Rihanna to ask the girls if the bottles had been opened before they made the punch, though sometimes it's hard to tell."

"It's worth a try." Jaxson leaned back in his chair. "What's next then?"

"We wait. I am curious what Nash reports about his interaction with Francine."

"I'm sure she'll have a perfectly good reason for being at the dance."

"Regardless, she'll have to admit that she lied to Kyle about not feeling well."

Jaxson shook his head. "She won't say she lied. Francine will claim she wanted to surprise him, though I'm not sure why she'd be dressed as a caterer. She certainly wouldn't say she was there to keep an eye on him."

I had to think about that. "Maybe, but she might not have had an excuse ready if she planned to kill him."

"True."

I turned on my computer, and for the first time in a long while, I wasn't sure what to do. Basically, I needed to think of a way to prove Francine was guilty, but how? The hard part was that time was running out. In two days, she'd return to California unless the sheriff's department had solid proof to keep her here.

When I had been stumped in the past, I often consulted with Gertrude. As soon as I thought of her, a lightbulb went off. Kyle might know who tried to kill him. Why not consult him? Sure, contacting a freshly dead person—was that even the right term?—was hit or miss. The deceased was often in shock at having been killed and might be on a mission for justice, unwilling or unable to communicate with the living. Even if he could connect with us, returning to speak to an old friend might not be high on the dead man's priority list, but I had to try.

I would have asked my mom to contact him, but she was busy arranging Kyle's funeral. I picked up my phone to make an appointment with Gertrude when I realized that we'd need more than just the two of us to do a séance. That meant I needed to wait for Rihanna to return from school to see if she'd join me. I might even have her ask Casi. Her friend was a witch, but it would be up to her if she wanted to have anything to do with speaking to the dead. After all, she had seen him die. I turned to Jaxson and told him of my plan.

"I like it," he said. "It will give Rihanna more practice, especially since you and Gertrude have been fairly successful in speaking with those who have passed over."

"I agree."

It wasn't very long before my cousin came home from school and tossed her backpack on the sofa. "You're excited," she announced.

"Did you read my mind? Because if you did, I won't need to explain anything."

Rihanna chuckled. "I didn't. Reading minds takes a lot of energy. Besides, I said I would try not to. No, you have this excess energy about you. Something must have happened."

That was a reasonable deduction. I told her about the

video.

"Francine killed Kyle?"

"I can't be sure, but she was at the reunion posing as a caterer. Could you ask Lena or Casi if they remember if the soda bottles had been opened before they made the punch? I have a theory I want to test."

"Sure." Rihanna dropped down onto the sofa and dialed one of the girls' numbers. "Casi. Can you remember if the soda bottles were opened before you made the punch...Uh-huh...No, that's okay."

I held up a finger to get Rihanna's attention.

"Hold on a sec, Casi."

"I'm thinking of asking Gertrude to conduct a séance to contact Kyle. Would you and or Casi like to join me?"

"I would. Let me ask her." My cousin explained what we wanted to do. Rihanna looked up at me. "When?"

"Hopefully today, but I need to call Gertrude. We'll have to call Casi back."

Rihanna relayed the message and then hung up. "Do you think he'll answer? I mean, Mr. Covington might not have any idea who wanted him dead. If he recognized Francine, wouldn't you have seen the interaction on tape?"

"Yes, but I figured she hid out of sight after she put the spell on the punch."

"That doesn't seem suspicious at all." Rihanna rolled her eyes.

"I know. Everyone has made the same comment." I called Gertrude.

"I'd be happy to help. I have an opening in an hour."

"Perfect. We'll be there."

Rihanna called Casi back, asking her to meet us in the lobby of the Psychics Corner. "She's super excited. It will be her first séance," Rihanna said.

"Will Lena be upset that you didn't call her?"

"Can I invite her?"

Aunt Fern's friends helped me with a séance even though they weren't witches. "Sure."

Even over the phone I could hear Lena's squeals of delight. I guess if my two friends had powers, I would have felt a bit left out. This would give her a chance to share in a magical experience.

"I'm feeling rather positive about this séance," Rihanna told me.

"Me, too."

When it was time to go, just as we approached the door to the outside, Iggy blocked our path. "Did you forget something?"

"What would that be?" I asked him.

If he had hips, he would have planted a hand on them. "Me."

He'd participated in two other séances. "You want to come?"

"Does a bear—"

"Uh, uh. I get it. Yes, you can come."

Since he was already wearing his sweater, he'd be warm enough for the short walk over. I placed him in my purse and headed out. When we arrived, we found both Casi and Lena in the lobby, chatting away.

"Are we really going to talk to the dead?" Lena asked.

I wanted to be honest. "A séance can take many forms.

The person contacted might appear as a ghost, talk through another person, communicate with only one person, or not show up at all."

Casi giggled. "I can't wait."

Fingers crossed this wasn't a bust. The four—or rather the five—of us headed to Gertrude's office. To my surprise, she already had the table set up and the candles lit.

"Right on time." She hugged Rihanna and me. "It's nice to see you ladies again. I'm sorry about what happened to Drake's friend."

"Thanks." I introduced Lena and Casi. "I don't have real high hopes that Kyle can tell us much, but maybe he can give us an idea who might have wanted to harm him. I really want to know if he has any idea if Francine has magical powers."

Gertrude nodded. "We'll see what we can do."

Once we sat at the table with Iggy between me and Rihanna, Gertrude gave the two newcomers instructions. "Are we ready?" she asked.

The excitement in the air was palpable. Gertrude inhaled and called upon Kyle Covington to speak. "Do you believe that Francine Xavier tried to poison you?"

When nothing happened, I sagged against my seat, but I didn't open my eyes or break contact with my fingers.

Just as I was about to declare this a bust, a deep voice came out of the blue. "She wouldn't do that. Not Francine."

"Who would have?" Gertrude asked as calm as could be.

"No one."

He was in denial, and that was a shame. Was Kyle even aware he was dead?

"What about Ronnie Taggert?" she asked. Yes, I'd

prepped her on the names of our suspects.

"Why would he want to harm me? I told him I could give him the money in a month. Just not now."

His story didn't match either Jude's or Francine's.

Asking a question now probably wouldn't hurt. "Does Francine have witch powers?"

I expected him to deny the claim instantly, but he didn't. "She might."

That was interesting. "Did you know she came to the dance pretending to be a caterer?"

"No way. Francine isn't sneaky. She loves me. I know she does."

I noted the use of present tense. Surely, he'd known their relationship wouldn't return to normal after he delayed their wedding. I saw no need to mention that now, however. "Did Jude like Francine a lot?"

A thump sounded. Oh, no. I hope the voice hadn't come through Gertrude. She was too old to be the conduit. I opened my eyes, only to find our resident psychic with her forehead on the table. "Rihanna?" My voice cracked.

My cousin had been working with Gertrude and had experienced her passing out a few times. She knew what to do.

Like a pro, Rihanna rushed over to the sink, ran some water on a towel, and carried it over. "Come on, Gertrude. Sit up for me."

Ever so gently, Rihanna leaned her back. Gertrude opened her eyes, but her mouth appeared a bit slack. "He came through me, didn't he?"

Had I not experienced the phenomenon myself, I wouldn't have believed the person who'd been channeled didn't remember much. "Yes, he did."

"Did he tell you anything of value?" she asked us.

When no one spoke up, I answered. "I'm not sure. Kyle didn't know who had harmed him, nor did he believe it could have been Francine. However, he admitted that she might have some powers."

Gertrude nodded. "Good. That's a start."

A start? I wasn't sure what that meant. "Do you think he'll be ready to say more later?"

She shrugged. "Every spirit is different."

Casi and Lena asked a few additional questions about the process, and then we left. I paid on the way out, and the whole time, both Casi and Lena didn't stop talking about their experience.

"That was so cool," Casi said. "Thank you for inviting us."

I was happy that the séance didn't spook her. "You're welcome, but please don't mention this to anyone. At least not until the killer is brought to justice."

Both girls seemed to understand. "For sure," Lena said.

I thanked them for rushing over and joining us. On the way back, Rihanna was rather quiet. "Is something bothering you?"

"Toward the end, I had the sense Kyle started to doubt Francine."

"What do you mean?"

"When you told him that Francine was at the dance but didn't tell him, I got a chill."

I stilled. "A chill, as in his ghost was in the room."

She looked over at me. "Exactly. I think he was trying to

tell me something, only I don't know what."

"Darn it. I should have opened my eyes." I unlatched my purse. "Iggy, did you see a ghost?"

"Are you asking if I cheated?"

I wouldn't put it past him. "I guess."

"Fine. I might have seen a white, hazy figure."

Really? "Why didn't you say something?"

"He couldn't have understood me even if I'd spoken."

I wasn't so sure. A non-witch couldn't understand Iggy, but who was to say the same rules applied to the dead? At the very least, Iggy should have nudged my hand with his leg to indicate something was happening.

"What is done is done. Let's hope Nash can find answers about why Francine was at the gym the night of the reunion."

No sooner had we entered the office when my cell rang. Jaxson looked up from the desk and smiled. I checked the caller ID. "It's Nash."

I slipped my bag off my shoulder and dropped onto the sofa.

Jaxson mouthed if I wanted some tea, and I nodded. He was the best.

"Hey, Nash."

"I just got back from the Magic Wand Hotel."

"What did Francine say?"

"You won't believe it."

Chapter Eleven

"WHAT WON'T I believe?" I asked.

"Francine has checked out of the hotel."

I motioned for Rihanna to sit next to me. "I'm putting you on speaker. Rihanna and Jaxson are here." Or at least he would be as soon as he returned with my drink.

"Sure."

"When did Francine leave the hotel, and did you learn why she left?"

"She checked out about an hour before I got there, and no, she didn't say why."

"The clerk at the hotel might have some information."

"I asked," he said. "But Francine didn't say. To be thorough, I called the airlines, but they had no record of a Francine Xavier boarding a plane or buying an airline ticket."

"I find it hard to believe she'd miss Kyle's funeral—unless she was the one who killed him. Or she went to a different hotel because it was cheaper. The expensive clothes might have been just for show."

"I imagine a Silicon Valley accountant could afford the Magic Wand Hotel."

"True. Did you contact Jude?" I asked.

"That was my next call."

I decided to tell Nash about our séance. He believed in curses and magic, so I didn't think he'd make fun of me if I recounted our contact with our dead man. "Because I wanted to find out if Kyle knew who might have killed him, Rihanna, myself, and her two girlfriends did a séance with Gertrude Poole to contact Kyle."

"Did he tell you anything?"

I appreciated that Nash sounded hopeful. "I'm not sure."

I told him as much of the conversation as I could remember. I turned to Rihanna and nodded. She then gave him her impression.

"From what you ladies are saying, Francine is still our number one suspect."

"Yes, but we have no proof of her involvement in Kyle's death."

"Let's hope we get lucky in the next two days then. If Jude knows anything, I'll contact you."

"Thank you."

I disconnected. Jaxson had returned with my iced tea and had it placed on the table. The first sip hit the spot.

"How does Francine's disappearance affect your thinking?" Jaxson asked.

"I'm not sure. I'm still trying to process it."

"Do you know if she rented a car? Or rather if Kyle rented a car?"

I smiled. "I see your logic. You're wondering if she returned the rental. That might tell us if she is on the run or not."

"Yes. How about texting Nash to see if he knows."

That was a good idea. If he hadn't thought of it, he'd find

the answer soon enough.

Just then, Drake came up the interior stairwell. "Hey guys. Glinda, have you heard from Andi in the last few hours?"

"No. She was at the store when we left. That's the last contact I've had with her."

"Me, too. Remember she made a motion indicating that I should call her? Well, I have been trying, but it keeps going to her voicemail."

I didn't think that all too odd. "She might have been with a customer."

"Four times?"

Jaxson looked over at me and rolled his eyes. "Why don't you walk over to the Hex and Bones and talk to her," he said.

Drake snapped his fingers. "Why didn't I think of that?" He huffed. "I was just over there. Elizabeth said that Andi received a call about an hour ago and then left. She has yet to return."

"Did she tell her cousin when she'd be back?" I asked.

"No."

"Aren't you two supposed to go out tonight?"

"Yes."

Drake was clearly upset. "What can I do?"

"Remember when Rihanna went missing, or rather when Mr. Plimpton kidnapped her?"

"Technically, I was already in his house when he locked me in his back room," my cousin added.

Drake waved a hand. "Whatever. Here's the thing. Glinda, you did a locator spell and found her."

I didn't want to mislead him. "I found Rihanna's car, not

Rihanna, but that led us to her. Andorra hasn't been gone very long. There could be a perfectly good explanation for why she's not answering."

"Elizabeth tried calling her, and even she couldn't get a hold of her."

That wasn't like Andorra. To prove to myself that Drake was just being paranoid, I called her, but I got the same result. "Maybe her cell battery ran out of juice. How about you and I head on over to the shop to see if Elizabeth has a suggestion as to where Andorra was headed? I'd hate it if she was stuck on some side road waiting for someone to drive by and rescue her."

"Thank you."

"Glinda," Jaxson said. "Do you think it's a coincidence that Andorra is missing just when Francine checks out of her hotel?"

My heart dropped to my stomach. "What are you implying?"

Jaxson held up both hands. "Nothing, but the timing seems odd."

"Francine is missing?" Drake asked.

I told him what Nash had said. "Do I think Francine might be involved in Kyle's murder? Yes, but what would that have to do with Andorra?"

His brows pinched. "Are you kidding me? We were asking questions about the murder at the bar. It wouldn't take a lot of well-placed questions to find out you are a sleuth."

"Me, sure, but not Andorra."

"She and her cousin, along with her grandmother, run a magic shop, for lack of a better name. What if Francine is a witch? She might fear Andi."

This was getting out of hand. "Let's see what Elizabeth has to say before we let our imaginations get the best of us."

Iggy peeked his head out from under the desk. He looked from me to Drake. "Do you want to come?" I asked.

"Other than Andorra, I'm the only one who can talk to Hugo."

"Then hop in my purse."

He waddled over to it. I lifted him up and placed him inside.

"Good luck," Jaxson said.

"Do you want me to be there?" Rihanna asked.

"If you want to." It was always helpful to have our lie detector with us. Memories of my best female friend rushed back. Penny Carsted couldn't read minds, but she was really good at knowing if someone lied.

Rihanna flashed me a brief smile, bringing me back to the present. "I do."

We all headed out. The Hex and Bones was empty when we walked in. Elizabeth was at the counter with the cash drawer out. She looked up. "Hey. I'm just closing."

That worked for me. "We're worried about your cousin," I said.

Elizabeth pulled the cash out of the drawers, saying nothing, which I found quite odd.

Iggy poked his head out from inside my bag. "I want to talk to Hugo."

I placed him on the floor. Elizabeth seemed so distracted that she probably wouldn't notice my iguana crawling around the counter and entering the back room.

"Is something wrong?" I asked her.

"No. I just need to count this money."

Rihanna placed a hand on mine and slightly shook her head, indicating Elizabeth wasn't telling the truth. "There's something you should know. Your cousin might be in trouble." I explained about Francine having checked out of the hotel. "Kyle's funeral isn't for another two days. I can't imagine his fiancée would up and leave."

"No. Neither do I."

I stepped closed to Elizabeth. "What aren't you telling us?"

"Please." Drake sounded at his wits end.

Elizabeth straightened. "You need to leave."

I didn't know Elizabeth very well, but this wasn't like her. "Tell us what you know."

"I don't know anything." Panic wavered on her words.

I might not read minds, but it was clear to me that she was still lying. "I'd like to do a locator spell to find Andorra."

Elizabeth perked up. "Yes, yes. That's good."

I didn't expect her sudden change of mood. What was going on with her? "Here's the thing. You need to do the spell since it has to be conducted by someone connected to Andorra. Your grandmother had me find Rihanna, because we were related."

"That makes sense." Elizabeth tapped her chin. "I know of this spell. I just need to find the list of ingredients, but first I should lock up. We don't need anyone coming in."

She rushed to the front, locked the door, and then raced to the back room. I motioned for Drake and Rihanna that we follow her. I also wanted to check up on Iggy to make sure he was okay.

When we stepped into the storage room, Iggy was on a table talking to Hugo, though talking wasn't quite the right word. It was a one-sided conversation. Iggy turned to us. "What's going on?"

"We're going to do a locator spell to find Andorra."

"Good idea. Can I help?"

"Thanks for asking, but since Elizabeth is close to her cousin, she'll be performing the spell." I turned to her. "Your grandmother said I had to hold something of Rihanna's."

My cousin touched my arm. "What did you use?"

"That photo of you and your mom."

She half-smiled. "I've always loved that picture of the two of us."

"Me, too."

Elizabeth pulled down a book and flipped through the pages, her eyes squinting and her mouth pinching.

I wanted to help. "I remember some of the ingredients, just not all of them. It will have dragon's blood sage with strands of the sweet grass sage. Bertha said it was used to bring harmony and protection to both of us during the locator spell. You'll also need four rocks."

Elizabeth nodded. "Thank you. That is helpful. I know which one that is now." It only took her a moment before she waved a book. "I found it."

She handed it to Rihanna and asked her to read the required ingredients out loud. Once Elizabeth placed the necessary items on the small table, she looked around.

Her frantic movements were ratcheting up my anxieties. "What do you need?" I asked.

"Something that belonged to my cousin. I don't want to take the time to drive home."

I helped check out the storeroom but saw nothing personal. When my gaze latched onto Drake, I smiled. "How about Drake here? You can have him sit next to you. She does cherish him."

It was like I'd released the anxiety from her body. "Yes, that's perfect."

Thankfully, Drake didn't argue. Elizabeth set out the four stones, each facing in a different direction. She then placed the herbs in the middle, and once she lit them, she fanned the smoke over the rocks, just like I had done.

I held my breath, hoping that one of the stones would glow, indicating where our friend might be. Elizabeth then closed her eyes. A few seconds later, the rock facing east pulsed with light. Drake reached up, grabbed my arm, and nodded to the lit rock, hope filling his eyes.

Elizabeth inhaled, clearly trying to connect to Andorra. After a full minute, she opened them and sank back. "I can't."

"Can't what?" I asked.

"Connect with her. It's as if there is an impediment between us."

Maybe having Drake sitting next to her wasn't enough.

"Let Hugo try," Iggy said.

"What do you mean?" I don't know why I asked. It made sense that Hugo might be successful since he and Andorra could communicate telepathically. "Hugo, can you talk to her even if she is far away?"

Iggy looked over at him. "I see." He faced me again. "No, he can't, but maybe with the spell, he can find her."

I faced Elizabeth. "Do you think it will work?"

"It's worth a try. We have to find her no matter what."

"Before he tries to find her, Hugo wants to know what you did," Iggy said.

She stilled. "Me?"

"Elizabeth," Rihanna said. "Hugo is right. I can tell you had no choice, but you need to come clean."

Her mouth opened. She took one look at Hugo and nodded. My own heart was beating so hard, I feared I might need to sit.

"This morning, I…ah…received a phone call from some person with a distorted voice."

The pieces fell into place. "Is that why you were acting a bit strange when you returned to the store?"

"Yes. I didn't have a doctor's appointment. I made that up."

Drake clasped her hand. "Tell us everything."

She inhaled. "The person on the phone told me to meet her—or maybe it was a man—in the park and said that if I told anyone, he'd hurt Andorra and my grandmother." Tears streamed down her cheeks.

"Who did you meet?" Drake asked.

"No one. When I got there and sat on the assigned bench, my phone rang." She pressed her lips together. "It was that same creepy voice."

"What did he want?" I asked.

"He told me to put a lethal spell on someone."

This was terrible. "Who were you to kill?"

"I can't tell you." She broke into tears once more, and my heart ached for her.

I suppose us knowing her assignment really didn't affect us finding Andorra. "How much time do you have before harm comes to your cousin?"

"Midnight tonight."

So soon? My stomach churned. "I trust you have no plans to fulfill this person's request?" I held my breath.

"No. I could never harm anyone. I tried to tell this person that, but he or she wouldn't listen. He kept saying the longer I took, more of my family would die—including me."

"Then we need to find Andorra first and keep her safe—along with you." I turned to Hugo. "What do you need to find her?"

Chapter Twelve

HUGO FACED IGGY. My iguana nodded a few times and then turned back to us. "He wants to try it without doing the spell first, but he'll need to hold something of Andorra's. He said a picture of her will do."

I wasn't sure how a picture would be more powerful than a spell, but who was I to second guess someone with Hugo's talents?

I looked over at Drake. "You must have a selfie of you two."

"I do. I do." He pulled out his phone and located a cute picture of them at the diner and held it up. They looked so happy. "Is this good enough?"

Hugo moved over and took the phone. He then nodded and closed his eyes. Since he couldn't talk, there was no way of knowing what he was doing, until he began to sway. If he'd been able to make a sound, I bet he'd be grunting or humming.

We waited a good minute or so for him to tell Iggy where she was. Hugo finally opened his eyes and turned to my familiar.

Iggy didn't have shoulders, but the muscles in his back sagged. "Hugo spoke with Andorra, but she seems to be in a trance. She doesn't know where she is or how she got there."

How terrible to be so close and yet so far away. "Hugo, can you ask Andorra to describe her surroundings? That might help us."

Hugo closed his eyes once more and seemed to be communicating with her. When he finished, he told Iggy, who then translated. "She's in a restaurant parking lot. That's all she knows, but she thinks she went there for some reason."

"To eat maybe?"

Hugo shrugged.

"Can she read the name of the restaurant?" Then we could find her.

He shook his head. Something must be blocking her abilities. I looked over at Elizabeth. "Is Andorra's car here?"

"No. I checked."

That almost implied she might have gone out to eat voluntarily. "Do you know of any spell that takes your will away?" If anyone knew, it would be Elizabeth.

She rocked back and forth in her chair. "Memaw mentioned one once. The person doing the spell merely had to make a suggestion, and the person under this curse would carry it out."

"Then why wouldn't this person perform this spell on you?" Drake asked. "She or he could make you kill the target, and you couldn't have stopped yourself."

She nodded. "You're right."

While all of this was helpful, we weren't any closer to finding Andorra. "We need to tell the sheriff. He can ask the neighboring sheriff departments to search for her. If Andorra is in or near her car, they should be able to find her."

"No!" Elizabeth said. "He'll arrest me."

"Why? You didn't harm anyone, did you?"

"No, but I should have reported the threatening phone call right away."

"You didn't know your cousin would be taken—or rather, would go missing."

She lowered her gaze. "No, I didn't."

"I bet Steve or Nash could look at the call log of your phone, as well as the one sent to Andorra's phone. It might tell us who called you."

Elizabeth pushed back her chair. "Maybe he can. If he needs it, I'll give him permission."

"Okay. Let's go." I turned to Hugo. "Do you want to add anything?"

I felt a little bad leaving him here, but Andorra said his strength came from the store. Hugo held up a hand and told Iggy his thoughts. "Hugo and I will stay here, but only if you remember to come get me afterward."

"I think you should come with us now. I have no idea how long it will take us to find Andorra."

Iggy turned back to Hugo and rubbed his head against the familiar's leg. Aw. That was so sweet. I was happy Iggy had found a new friend—odd though Hugo might be.

"Hugo wishes us luck."

"Thank you, Hugo."

Rihanna touched my arm. "I'm going to head back. I'll fill Jaxson in on what has happened."

"I appreciate it. Tell him I'll be back when I can." I figured she had homework to do anyway.

After securing Iggy in my purse, we went to the sheriff's

office. To my delight, both Nash and Steve were there. When we told them that Andorra was missing, they ushered us into the conference room.

"Tell us everything," Steve said.

Elizabeth went first, informing him of the calls that both she and Andorra had received. "This person wanted me to do a death spell. I imagine it would be like the one done on Kyle. I know I should have told you right away, but they said if I told the cops that they would kill Andorra and then my grandmother. I was really scared for my family."

"I understand," Steve said.

"I wouldn't be here now, except that Andorra is kind of missing, and we need your help to find her."

"Only kind of missing? What do you mean?" Nash asked.

Now it was my turn to explain. Andorra might not want the world to know about Hugo, but he was integral to this case. "I know you probably won't believe a familiar, but I have seen Andorra and Hugo communicate without talking."

"A familiar? Like Iggy?"

No one was like Iggy. Hugo would be hard to explain. "Close. When Hugo senses danger, he turns from a stone gargoyle statue into a human. Weird, I know. Even Andorra doesn't really understand him. What I do know is that he is mute, and only Andorra and Iggy can communicate with him. He was able to mentally connect with her, but Andorra doesn't know where she is other than at some restaurant parking lot."

Steve looked over at Elizabeth. "Can you corroborate this?"

"Yes."

"Okay. Did Andorra tell you the name of this restaurant?"

"No." If she had, we'd have jumped in our car and gone after her.

"I can ask the phone company to ping her location, assuming her phone is turned on. Even still, it will take time." Steve copied down her number as well as Elizabeth's. "I'll be right back to see what I can learn."

I looked over at Nash. "If we can believe this mystery caller, we only have until midnight tonight before harm comes to Andorra."

"That doesn't give us much time. Are you still thinking this is Francine's doing?"

"I have no proof, but I can't think of anyone else."

Nash turned to Elizabeth. "You need to tell me the target so we can protect this person."

She nodded. "That's the problem. It's Francine."

"What?" I hadn't expected that. "I thought she was the killer. I trust this person didn't say why she wanted Francine Xavier dead?"

"No."

Nash nodded. "We need to ask Jude Watson to come in. He might have a clue as to what in the world is going on."

"He claimed to know nothing before. Why would he know something now? Let's hope he isn't in cahoots with Francine," I mumbled.

"You think he is?"

I actually had given it some thought yesterday. "I can't say one way or the other." I looked from Drake to Elizabeth. She hadn't even met Jude, so she wouldn't be able to judge.

"I say we ask him to come here," Drake said. "However,

we should be cautious about how much we tell him."

"I'm okay with that, but things aren't lining up," I said.

"In what way?" Nash asked.

"I'm not saying I'm wrong about Francine poisoning Kyle. After all, she was the one who pretended to be a caterer. What I'm not sure about is who made Andorra drive to some parking lot? Francine would never ask Elizabeth to kill her—and by her, I mean Francine herself."

"I agree with you." Nash pulled out his phone and scrolled through a list. "I'll tell Jude to come over now."

"Listen to any background noise. He could be with Francine. They seem to be tight."

Nash smiled. "Here's a little secret. As soon as I found out that Francine had checked out of the hotel, I had Steve ask Sheriff Willows in Liberty to have one of her men watch Jude for that very reason."

Okay, I was impressed. "That was smart. You were one step ahead of me."

Nash tapped his head. "Sometimes magic isn't always needed."

"Touché."

He dialed Jude and asked if he could come to the station right away. "There has been a development in the Kyle Covington case...I'll discuss it when you get here. Thanks." Nash leaned back. "Now we wait."

"Did Jude say if he was at the hotel?" I asked.

"I didn't ask him. To answer your next question, I imagine he is aware that Francine is no longer in the room next to him."

"The last time I spoke with the two of them, they were

headed to the funeral home to discuss Kyle's service." I snapped my fingers. "Let me call Mom to see if they were telling the truth. That might let us know if at least one of them was on the up and up."

Nash nodded. "Good plan."

I spoke with my mother and briefly explained what was going on. "Did they show up?"

"Yes, but the meeting was brief."

"The service will still be in two days, right?" I don't know why I asked. My mom was always on time.

"Yes. What's wrong, sweetie?"

It would take too long to explain. "It's complicated. Drake and I are at the sheriff's office trying to find Francine. She's checked out of her room. Did she happen to say anything about that?"

"No, she didn't, but you could ask that nice young man with her."

"We intend to. Thanks, Mom."

From my conversation, I was sure they knew what had been discussed. As I turned to ask about Jude, the station's front door opened. From where I was sitting, I had a direct line of sight. Not only did Jude walk in, but Andorra was right behind him. What the heck? How was that possible?

I pushed back my chair so fast, it nearly tumbled. "Andorra's here."

My mind splintered. Had Jude taken her? If not, why was he with her?

Nash stood. "Stay here. All of you."

Steve must have heard Nash rush out of the conference room, because he came out of his office and halted when he saw our missing person. I couldn't hear what they were saying, but I figured we'd learn soon enough.

Drake stood. "I don't care what Nash says, I have to find out if Andorra is okay."

If that had been Jaxson or Rihanna, I would have gone out, too. I looked over at Elizabeth. Tears were trickling down her cheeks, only this time they seemed to be ones of joy.

"She's safe. I can't believe Andorra is safe," she mumbled.

"She is." I stepped over to the anxious woman and rubbed her shoulder, wanting her to be assured that she wasn't alone. "I was remiss in not asking where your grandmother is now?"

"She's in Missouri visiting her sister."

"Then she's safe, too."

Elizabeth nodded. I kept watching the rather odd scene in the main area unfold. Jennifer, who was at the reception desk, jumped up after Steve said something to her. He must have asked her to fetch some water or coffee. Once she retrieved the drink, she handed it to Andorra. Both officers then led the group to the conference room.

As Andorra approached, I tried to detect if she needed medical aid. Except for the rather vacant stare, she appeared unharmed.

When everyone entered the room, Drake led Andorra over to us and placed her between himself and Elizabeth. Steve, Nash, and Jude sat across from us.

"Tell us again where Andorra was when you arrived at the station," Steve asked Jude.

"She was just standing there, staring at the front door. I've never seen anything like it before."

I had to admit, Andorra seemed to be in a trance, like

Hugo claimed.

Drake lifted the untouched cup of water from her fingers and placed it on the table. He then clasped her hand. "Andi, can you tell us what happened?"

"I don't remember." Her voice sounded robotic.

"Were you with Francine?" Drake was so gentle with her.

"I don't remember."

I wondered if Andorra had been programmed to say that one phrase. "Elizabeth, do you know of something that might break her out of this brain fog?"

Her eyes widened. "No, but I can call Memaw."

"Great. Do that." Bertha usually had the answer to our witch dilemmas.

Elizabeth excused herself and stepped out of the room. Steve asked Andorra a few more questions, as did Nash, but nothing seemed to get through to her.

Jude turned to me. "You mentioned Francine. Have you seen her?"

"The last time was when she was with you, and you two were on your way to the funeral home."

"Jude, Francine checked out of her room," Nash said. "Do you know why?"

He glanced to the side. "No, but I can guess."

"Please do," Nash said.

"I might have said a few things that upset her—but not enough to make her leave."

"What did you say to her?" Steve asked.

"It had nothing to do with Kyle or his murder. It was personal."

I bet it was. "Did she ask if you cared for her?"

It looked like I'd punched him in the chest. "Kind of, yes. How did you know?"

"It makes sense, but tell me this. After Kyle told her that he wanted to delay their wedding, how did Francine react toward him?"

He pressed his lips together. "She was angry, but who wouldn't be?"

"Exactly. Did you ask Kyle why he sprang that decision on her? I'm assuming Francine hadn't expected it."

Jude blew out a breath. "She most definitely did not. Kyle did it, because he wanted to be certain that she loved him for who he was and not for his money. Was that corny? Sure, but that was Kyle. He was a sincere person."

A sincere person who wasn't the best judge of character. "Here's the thing. I know she worked for you, but can we assume she was interested in a better lifestyle?" I was trying to be tactful.

"Sure. Many people in Silicon Valley seem to be."

"Could it be that she thought she might have more luck with the other partner in the company?"

Jude's mouth opened and then quickly shut. "You mean me?"

The one and only. "Yes, you."

"It never occurred to me that she was interested—until she told me today."

That meant she was being subtle and possibly calculating. "Do you know where Kyle's phone is?"

"We have it." Steve answered instead. "Why?"

"By any chance did a Patricia Haltern call him or text him in the recent past?"

"Jaxson asked me that, but I don't have Patricia's number. It would take a long time to cross-reference all of Kyle's recent calls. If you know where she lives, that will really help."

"I don't know, but Kim Lucas should have that information."

"She doesn't. Patricia didn't provide a number."

That was too bad. Elizabeth came back inside. "I spoke with my grandmother, but she wasn't sure what to do. She said all we can do is be supportive and hope Andorra snaps out of it. In the meantime, my grandmother will research it."

I had to admit I was disappointed in that response. I looked over at Andorra, and my heart ached.

"Elizabeth, your cousin called Patricia recently. Can you check Andorra's phone and look at her recent calls? I'm hoping to get Patricia's number so Steve can compare it to Kyle's phone log."

"Sure." She placed a hand on Andorra's shoulder, but when her cousin didn't respond, Elizabeth looked over at me for direction.

"I'm sure she won't mind."

Andorra kept her phone in a small over-the-shoulder bag. Elizabeth slipped it out and handed it to me. I then gave it to Steve.

"I'll check it out right now," he said.

Chapter Thirteen

STEVE HADN'T BEEN gone but a minute when Elizabeth's phone rang. She jerked, indicating her nerves were on edge.

"Go ahead and answer it. It might be your grandmother." Hopefully, she'd found something to help Andorra.

"Yes, yes." She checked the screen, and her shoulders sagged. She nodded and answered. "Hey, Memaw. Did you find out anything?…Really?…Okay."

They talked for another minute and then she disconnected. "What did she say?" I asked.

"This is going to sound crazy, but she found something useful online, no less. The way to stop the trance is with a kiss."

A kiss? That was what transported Jaxson and me to another time. We didn't want that to happen here, but maybe when two people who deeply care for each other kissed, it could alter things. "Drake? What are you waiting for?"

I had to assume they'd kissed before, but from his reaction, maybe they hadn't.

He cupped Andorra's face. "Please come back to me. I miss you." Drake leaned over and pressed his lips to hers.

I held my breath, waiting and hoping, but telling myself

there was no way this could work.

When Drake leaned back, he stroked her cheek. "Andorra, can you hear me?" he asked.

One second she was staring, and the next, she sat up and looked around. "What's going on?"

I don't know who started it, but we all clapped. "You're at the sheriff's department, so you are safe," he said.

Her brows pinched in confusion. "How did I get here?"

Drake took her hands. "We were hoping you could tell us. We believe someone put a spell on you."

"A spell? Who?"

This wasn't getting us anywhere. "What's the last thing you remember, Andorra?" I asked.

She bit down on her lip. "I was at our store with you and Drake. You'd just met Hugo. As you were leaving, Elizabeth came back to the store, and then you left."

I refused to believe her own cousin would put a spell on her, or had she? Maybe Elizabeth had in order to keep her safe, but why not say so? We would have understood. "Elizabeth, can you tell us again what went down after we left the store?"

She nodded. "Like I said, Andorra received a phone call, but I didn't hear what was said, because I was with a customer."

That kind of implied Elizabeth wasn't involved, assuming she was telling the truth about being with a customer. "Do you remember this customer?" I didn't want to sound accusatory, but a person's life might be at stake.

She pressed her lips together. "A mother and her daughter. They were tourists. I can't imagine they'd have done anything to Andorra. They didn't even know her or so I assumed."

I was impressed with her good memory. "It is possible they'd been paid to do a spell. A mother daughter team would be a good cover."

"I guess."

"Andi, do you remember what was said in this call?" Drake asked.

She studied the ceiling and then blew out a breath. "Only that I needed to get into my car and drive east."

Excitement raced through me. That was the direction the locator spell indicated. "Did you recognize the voice?"

"No, but it sounded like a computer to me."

That might have been the same person who'd called Elizabeth. "How did you know when to park and where?"

She looked off to the side for a moment. "I don't know. I mean, I must have known, because I'm here now."

Her logic was a bit faulty, but I didn't see any purpose in pointing that out. Drake took hold of her hands again, lifted her fingertips to his lips, and lightly kissed them. I held my breath, waiting for another revelation to appear. Unfortunately, Andorra wasn't able to remember anything else.

We'd asked Jude here, and then Andorra's appearance made us take a detour, but this was the sheriff department's investigation—not mine. I nodded to Nash to indicate I had nothing more to ask Andorra.

"Jude," Nash said. "After you headed back to the hotel with Francine, she blurted out that she cared for you. You said that took you by surprise. Why?"

"Because she was the love of Kyle's life. It was why I

didn't think of her in that way. When I told her that, she got kind of upset. A moment later, she said she felt a chill come over her."

A chill? I wonder if it was Kyle's ghost. I'd ask, but he wouldn't know.

"Then what did you do?" Nash asked.

If Jude was innocent, I felt sorry for him being interrogated like this.

"I thought she might be coming down with something, so I watched her go into her room before I went into mine. I had a lot of thinking to do now that Kyle was gone, so I put the television on and took a shower."

It was all logical. If Nash went to the hotel a short while later, I had to hand it to Francine. She was a quick packer. She might have figured that she'd have to leave town quickly and was ready to go.

Or had she recognized that the cold chill came from Kyle who was trying to contact her, and she decided it was time to leave? That being said, the only way to know that was if she was a witch. But why be afraid of a ghost? It wasn't as if he could hurt her. Or could he? I had to admit, I wasn't an expert on the subject.

"Francine checked out of the hotel shortly thereafter," Nash said to Jude. "Did she tell you where she was going?"

"Francine never told me anything. I knocked on her door around two, and when she didn't answer, I figured she was resting. After our little conversation, I thought it best to let it be."

That made sense, also. "Any idea where she might have gone?" I asked.

"No. How would I? I'm not from around here," Jude said.

"Neither is Francine. Did she know anyone in town?"

He studied his fingers for a moment. "I think she came to Witch's Cove two Christmases ago with Kyle."

"To meet his parents?" I asked.

"Yes."

I turned to Nash. "Could she have gone to their home?" Wherever that was. I didn't even know if his parents still lived in town or not.

"His parents aren't home. They're on the cruise, remember?" Jude said.

"What better place to hide out than where no one will bother you?"

"How would she get in?" Jude asked.

Really? "Break a window? Or plead to a neighbor that she came all the way out here to surprise Kyle only to find out he had been murdered? I don't know. She could make up any kind of story. Francine seems like the persuasive type. I imagine a neighbor might have a spare key in case of emergency since the parents were on a cruise."

"I'll check it out," Nash said and then stood.

Just then, the front door to the station opened. This was a very busy place today. At first, I didn't recognize the person, and then I realized who it might be.

Jennifer greeted her and then escorted my former classmate into Steve's office. I turned to Andorra. "If I'm not mistaken, that was Patricia Haltern."

Andorra had been watching her. "It is, but what is she doing here?"

"She might have information about Kyle's death."

"Maybe."

I looked over at Nash who held up a hand. "I know what you're going to ask, and I agree. I'll see what she knows. Everyone wait here."

As soon as Nash disappeared, I turned back to Andorra. "Did Patricia ever hint she thought her husband wanted to harm Kyle?"

"No. He didn't want Patricia to come, sure, but she never said why."

"Is this Patricia woman the one you mentioned to me as having dated Kyle in high school?" Jude asked.

"Yes. She married within a year of graduating. I didn't keep up with her after that, but Andorra did for some time."

Andorra held up a hand. "Once she married Harry, Patricia never took any of my calls, so I stopped trying."

"That had to have been tough," I said.

A few minutes later, Steve and Nash returned with Patricia. Something bad must have happened, because she wouldn't meet either my gaze or Andorra's.

Steve motioned that Patricia take a seat. "Most of you know Patricia Haltern."

"I've not had the pleasure," Jude said, "but Glinda mentioned you and Kyle used to date in high school."

"We did."

Steve copied something from Patricia's phone onto his laptop. "Let me play this video that Patricia took the night Kyle died."

The video started off with the view of the gym. Then it looked as if Patricia was filming and walking at the same time.

She panned the room once more and then returned her aim to one corner—the corner where the fake caterer was standing. Francine didn't even seem to be aware Patricia was there, let alone had a phone in her hand, probably because Francine was focused on the table that held the punch. While the video didn't show who was at the table, if I had to guess, I'd say it was Kyle.

Then Francine started to speak. The noise from the party made it impossible to hear the words, but Patricia zoomed in enough to see Francine's lips move. Only because I suspected Francine of being a witch, did I believe she was performing a spell—a very lethal one. It only lasted about fifteen seconds before a crash sounded across the room. Someone screamed, and then Francine turned around and left. So much for being in love with Kyle Covington.

"She killed him," I said.

"Glinda, I understand you drawing that conclusion," Steve said, "but even you have to agree that no court of law would convict Francine of any wrong doing. She wasn't anywhere near Kyle."

He had to say that. "Then we'll need to get proof," I announced.

Andorra perked up. "Why were you filming a caterer?"

I was glad Andorra brought that up, in part because it indicated she was mentally present—a lot more than I was.

"I'm ashamed to admit that I kind of stalked Kyle when he arrived in Witch's Cove."

"Did your husband know?" I couldn't help but ask.

"Of course not. I told him I was going to visit Andorra, and he believed me since we had been friends. Instead, I sat in the Magic Wand Hotel lobby waiting for a glimpse of Kyle. Sad to say, he didn't acknowledge me when he and Francine walked by. When I saw him with her, I will admit that I was quite jealous. Just look at her. She's beautiful and perfect. And me? After two kids, I've let myself go. I don't know why I even thought Kyle might look at me after all these years, but I had to find out."

"Your marriage wasn't the best, I take it?" I imagine it was a sore subject, but it might be cathartic for her to talk about it.

"You have no idea. I loved Kyle—or at least I thought I did. Eighteen-year-olds aren't always the best judges of character. After Kyle went to Harvard, I was lost. I went to community college where I met Harry. He was really understanding at first, and I was so lonely that I fell for him." She shook her head. "I was a fool. I don't need to go into the details of how controlling he became, and even though we have two children together, I wanted to leave him. The problem was that I had no money. I'd begged him to let me get a job, but he refused. Without funds, I couldn't leave—and he knew that."

Her story was one I'd heard before. "I'm sorry."

"Me, too," Andorra said. "I tried to call, but Harry wouldn't let me talk to you."

"I know."

"Tell us, Mrs. Haltern, why exactly did you videotape Francine?" Steve asked.

I was glad he brought us back to the topic at hand.

"It was probably stupid and a bit hopeful. I wanted to see what the woman who was with Kyle was really like. I followed her the day of the dance, and when I found out she went to a caterer, I was confused."

"I can see why," Steve said. "Go on."

"I followed her to the dance, too. When I spotted her standing in the corner, I saw my chance to show Kyle what kind of woman she was. His perfect woman wasn't so perfect."

"You had no problem recognizing her with the blonde wig?" I asked.

"No. Like I said, I followed her from the catering place. I don't know where she got the uniform, but she didn't put the wig on until after she arrived at the gym."

That made sense. "Your plan then was to show Kyle the video of Francine dressed up. Were you hoping that he would say what a fool he'd been and ask you to stay with him?"

In a way, Drake had taken one look at Andorra and thought the exact thing.

"I guess."

"And your husband?" Nash asked.

"I would have left him. He has no interest in me anymore or in our kids."

My sympathies swelled. "That has to be tough."

"It is."

"What did you do when you saw Kyle collapse?" Steve asked.

"I freaked. I wanted to go to him, but just at that moment, Harry came over and asked what I was doing."

"You had to say nothing, right?" I asked.

She dipped her chin. "I couldn't say anything."

When no one asked her any more questions, Steve escorted her out. My mind reeled after that sad tale. I was certain that Francine had said some kind of spell. Until we knew exactly what it was, we'd never be able to track it down to see if she'd meant for Kyle to die.

"Do we know anyone who can read lips?" I asked those present.

"Hugo can read lips," Andorra said. "Don't ask me how, though."

I turned to Nash. "Can we get a copy of the tape so we can find out exactly what Francine said?"

"I was hoping you'd ask."

Chapter Fourteen

JUDE SAT AT the table, seemingly stunned. "I knew that Francine was a bit deceptive, but Kyle loved her. I can't believe she might have killed him—assuming she was saying some kind of spell." He faced us. "Are you sure magic could do this?"

I could have given him a list of the times magic had been used to harm another, but I didn't see the point. "Yes. Andorra and I worked with the medical examiner, and even she agrees that is what killed him."

He whistled. "It's going to take a while to process this."

"I understand."

Steve returned and sat down. "That was unexpected."

"No kidding," I shot back.

"By the way," Steve said to me, "I followed up on the phone logs. Patricia and Kyle hadn't chatted prior to his arrival."

"They could have chatted on social media, though. Did you ever get the photos Jaxson asked for?" I asked.

"Yes. I'll send them to Jaxson."

And Jaxson would forward them to Elizabeth to see if she recognized anyone purchasing the ingredients for the spell. At this point in the investigation, I wasn't sure how much it could help, but it would show who might be involved.

"Thanks."

Once Nash made us a copy of Patricia's video and placed it on a flash drive, all of us, except for Jude, went back to Hex and Bones. Because he was so upset, and he didn't possess any magic, I saw no reason to burden him further. Drake wasn't a warlock, but Andorra needed him by her side.

I was sure that Nash would follow up on locating Francine, who hopefully was at Kyle's parents' home. As soon as we entered the store, I let Iggy loose. Elizabeth unlocked the back room, and he raced inside. A second later, Iggy came out. "Hugo isn't there."

"What?" Andorra said. She rushed to the back. "Hugo?" she called.

Even though I was curious to know what was going on, I wanted to give her a minute to check thoroughly. Andorra finally came out. "Hugo has retreated to his gargoyle state."

Darn. "What causes him to change back into human form?"

"Danger."

"Does that mean he thinks you and your family are out of danger? Is that why he returned to his original form?"

She nodded.

Drake turned to Andorra and rubbed her arm. "I'm not buying it, Andi. You and Elizabeth still need to be careful. We don't know who is behind your recent mind-controlling event. When midnight comes and Francine isn't dead, this person might come after you. Can't you ask Hugo to return to his human form so he can help us with the spell?"

"I can ask, but I know he won't change back without

good cause."

Drake stepped closer and pulled her into a hug. "Don't worry. I'll keep you safe."

That was so sweet, but what about Elizabeth? She was in equal danger. I turned to her. "You can stay with me tonight. I don't want you to be alone."

Drake shook his head. "No. I have a two-bedroom place. You and Andorra can stay in the spare bedroom."

Elizabeth let out a long breath. "That would be great. Thank you."

Iggy looked up at me. I picked him up, knowing he was disappointed his new friend had retreated into his old self.

"It's okay," he said. "I'm sure there are other people who can read lips."

"There are." At least I hoped there were.

"Do you know of someone?" Elizabeth asked me.

"I might." I explained about Levy and his coven. "Their talents are vast. Let me give him a call to see if he can help. He's Gertrude Poole's grandson."

"Ah. That means he has powerful genes."

I smiled. "He does." I pulled out my phone and called him. It took a few minutes to explain about Kyle's death and the spell. "We have the witch on tape, but we can't hear what she is saying. Do you know of anyone who can read lips?"

"Give me an hour, and I'll call you back."

"You are the best." I told them what Levy said.

"Then we wait." Andorra rubbed her stomach. "Is anyone up for a trip to the diner? I'm starving. I haven't eaten all day."

I smiled. "I can hear a chocolate shake calling my name.

Besides, being in public would make it less likely he'd do any of us harm." As we walked over there, I called Jaxson and briefly filled him in. "We're heading to the diner. Care to join us? And ask Rihanna, though she might be busy with school work."

"Actually, Gavin called."

"She's meeting him, I take it?" I shouldn't be worried about her, but I was, even though Rihanna always seemed to have everything under control.

"Yes, so you're stuck with just me."

"I'll never consider being with you as stuck."

He chuckled and disconnected. Once we went inside the Spellbound Diner, we slipped into a booth for six, just as Dolly rushed over. "I heard you all have been busy."

There was no way she could have learned anything about Patricia's video or the spell put on Andorra so quickly. Pearl, her usual source at the sheriff's office, wasn't even working today. "We did."

"Any leads on who killed Kyle Covington?"

It seemed as if she was a bit behind in the gossip. "Some. How about we order and then chat?"

Dolly grinned and pulled out her pad. "What will you have?"

We ordered quickly, and she disappeared, no doubt anxious to learn what we knew. If she had any knowledge about Patricia or Francine, I was willing to share a bit.

In short order, Dolly returned with our drinks. Since she knew a lot, I thought I'd ask her to help us with our immediate plight. "By any chance, do you know of anyone who can read lips?"

"Dave Sanders' sister can."

Dave owned the dive shop next to Drake's store.

"Of course," Drake said. "She was born deaf but had cochlear implants imbedded about five years ago."

Dolly nodded. "Yes, and even though she can now hear, she reads lips very well."

I smiled. "That is very helpful. Thank you."

"Why did you need that talent?"

Since she'd provided us with something valuable, I thought it only fair to give her something back. "Apparently, someone at the reunion was videotaping the festivities, and she caught someone on tape doing what looked like a spell. Seconds later, Kyle dropped to the floor."

Dolly sucked in a breath. "Kyle Covington died by the hand of a witch?"

"We think so."

"Do you know who did it?" she asked.

Even though two witches might be involved in this whole sordid event, I was sure Francine was one of them. However, if she found out the whole town was aware of her guilt, she might run. "Not at the moment."

Even if Dave's sister could translate the spell, it wouldn't bring Kyle back nor would it convict Francine. It would merely confirm—at least to us—that Francine was guilty. As Jaxson would say: one step at a time.

She smiled briefly. "Well, if I hear of anything, I'll let you know."

"I appreciate it."

A crowd entered the diner, and Dolly was suddenly swamped. She rushed off to take care of them.

We briefly chatted about our options and had mostly finished our meal when Levy called me back.

"Yes?" I might have sounded overly anxious, because…well…I was.

"I'm sorry, but I couldn't find anyone to help you."

I told him about the sister of one of the local merchants. "If she can translate it, can I email you the spell? All we need to know is the spell's intent. Is it supposed to be lethal or not?"

Heaven only knew, I'd tried some spells that ended up doing something different than planned.

"Of course."

"I owe you once more."

"Nonsense. What are friends for if not to help each other?"

Levy was the best. Once I disconnected, I turned to Drake. "Could you call Dave and ask if his sister can help us?" He and Dave were friends.

"Sure."

The conversation was short and to the point. When Drake finished, he faced us, and smiled. "His sister, Blythe, would be thrilled to help."

"Great. Where and when can we meet?"

"Dave said they could meet us at your office in fifteen minutes."

"Fantastic."

We finished our meal, and as we checked out, I bought some cookies for dessert. No good deed should go unrewarded. Thankfully, we arrived before Dave and his sister did, which gave Jaxson enough time to set up the video.

We watched it again, but I couldn't make heads or tails of it. With little time to spare, Dave and his sister arrived, and if I had to guess, Blythe was maybe twenty-two, pretty, and seemed a bit shy. I introduced her to the group and then led her over to the computer. "At times, the woman turns her head away from the camera."

Blythe sucked in a breath. "I don't think I can help then."

"Whatever words you can figure out will help."

"I've never done anything like this before, but I'll try."

Jaxson placed a pad of paper and a pencil in front of her. "This button can slow the video down."

Blythe looked up and smiled. "Thank you."

Since we didn't want to hover over her and make her any more nervous than she probably already was, we returned to the sofa. The spell wasn't more than maybe five sentences, so it shouldn't take her too long. Or so I hoped.

Blythe played the same few sentences over and over again. After fifteen minutes, she turned off the video and came over.

"This is the best I could do." She handed me the paper.

"That's awesome. Better than I could have hoped for."

I motioned she sit and enjoy the cookies while Elizabeth, Andorra, Rihanna, and I looked over the spell. Between the four of us, I was hoping we could spot something that indicated death was the goal.

It was Andorra who noticed it first. "Here is where it indicates that the ingredients need to combine."

"To something lethal, though?" I asked.

She shook her head. "I don't know."

"We need to ask Levy," Rihanna said.

I turned to Blythe and then Dave. "Thank you so much.

You might have helped bring a murderer to justice."

Both were quite excited that they'd had the chance to help. When they left, I typed the words of the spell—or what we know of them—into a message and emailed it to Levy.

"Let's say Levy's coven finds the exact spell," Rihanna said. "Furthermore, suppose they say that it was a spell designed to kill. It won't hold up in court, will it?"

I was no lawyer, but even I knew the answer. "No. We'll have to figure out a way to get Francine to confess." Rihanna rolled her eyes, and I couldn't blame her. "As for who wanted Andorra out of the way for a few hours, we'll have to tackle that later."

Elizabeth held up a finger. "Could Francine have asked that I kill her to throw us off track, so we'd think another person was involved?"

"I kind of doubt it since you might have been successful. I forgot to ask where you were supposed to execute this death sentence?"

"At the Magic Wand Hotel."

"Which she conveniently checked out of."

"That means Francine could have orchestrated it," Andorra said.

"Maybe, but something doesn't seem right." I tried to picture how this spell would go down but couldn't. "Elizabeth, did this person tell you what to say to Francine? I can't imagine if a complete stranger knocked on my hotel door, asking to be let in, that I'd welcome her with open arms. Or did the person expect you to do a spell in the lobby?"

"No. In her room, which was why I was to tell Francine that I heard she might need a foolproof love spell."

I nearly spit out my tea. "You didn't tell this to us before, why?" That might have come out too harsh.

"Once you told me Andorra was missing, I forgot everything." Elizabeth visibly shook.

"I'm sorry. You did nothing to deserve this," I said. "Did this distorted voice tell you who Francine wanted you to put the love spell on?"

"No. I was merely to tell her that the spell would take place in two parts. One was to be put on her and the other on the man she wanted to love her back. Unbeknownst to Francine, the first spell would kill her. I just hoped she wasn't talented enough to see through my ruse."

I thought about that for a bit. "It is quite ingenious. I assume you know how to do this spell?" It seemed very complicated to me.

"No. The voice thought I would, though, since I was a witch."

"How did this person know you were one?" Drake asked.

Elizabeth shrugged. "I work at an occult store. They must have assumed I was."

"A witch would know that wasn't how it worked," I said.

"I agree with Glinda," Andorra said. "I also find it odd that this person would assume Francine would fall for a spell of this kind."

"That kind of implies the funny-voiced person didn't know that Francine was a witch," Drake threw in.

"You're right," I said. "While all of this is great information, it doesn't help us prove that Francine is a killer. Whoever tried to have Francine killed should be our secondary concern. If you want to go after this distorted-voice person first, okay, but I don't know where to start." I looked around.

"I agree with Glinda. Let's prove Francine killed Kyle first," Andorra said. "Then we can tackle the second issue."

"Great. How? All suggestions, no matter how strange, are welcome," I said.

Andorra inhaled. "We need a truth spell."

I'd never heard of one, but that didn't mean one didn't exist. "Short of trying to find some sodium pentothal—assuming that chemical is actually used in places other than the movies—what kind of spell makes a person tell the truth?" I asked.

"We can ask Levy," Rihanna said.

I waited for other suggestions, but no one said anything. "Okay. We'll ask Levy for a truth spell. That's one more favor I'll owe him. First and foremost is finding Francine, though. Then we'll have to figure out a way to put the spell on her."

"We'll ask Jude to help," Jaxson offered.

"What can he do? He's no warlock."

Jaxson chuckled. "I'm thinking he can sweet-talk Francine into doing what we want."

That made sense. "If she wants him as a partner, she probably will do what he asks. Good thinking. And if Jude wasn't part of the plot to kill his business partner, I would think he'd want to see justice served for his friend."

"Great high-level thinking. Let's talk logistics," Drake said.

Logistics? I loved it. "Let's do it."

My good friend smiled. "If Francine is at Kyle's parents' house, we need Nash to stand down."

"I agree that we can't do much if she is in jail. Are you suggesting we ask Nash not to bring her in for questioning?"

"For now, yes."

"Then what?" I asked.

Rihanna stood. "I think it's time for the white board. This could get complicated fast."

Pride swelled. I'd taught her well. "Great. Logistics aside, we definitely need a truth spell."

Elizabeth stood. "Come to think of it, I might know of one, but I'll call Memaw to make sure and then check our ingredients." She turned to Andorra. "Do you want to come with me to the store? I don't want to walk outside alone."

"Sure."

"I'll escort you ladies." Drake stood and faced us. "Do you think you, Jaxson, and Rihanna can come up with a plan?"

I did adore him. "It's what we do."

"Then we'll be in the store waiting for further instructions."

No pressure. "I'll call Levy to see if he knows of a spell, too. In the meantime, you look for one. Once we have it, we'll figure out a way to get Francine to the Hex and Bones so we can administer it."

Easy peasy. Or not.

Chapter Fifteen

WITH MY WHITE board pen in hand, I looked at my two cohorts. "What is step one?"

"Call Nash and tell him to locate Francine but not apprehend her," Jaxson said.

"Okay, but I hope he'll agree."

Rihanna nodded. "He should. Both Nash and Steve realize that this is a witch-driven crime. They need us. If you explain about wanting to do a truth spell on Francine, I don't think they'll interfere."

I pulled out my phone. "Let's see if they found her first. If they don't know where she is, then it will be hard to proceed."

I called Nash since he was the one who said he'd locate her. "Hey, Glinda. No, I haven't brought Francine in yet."

"Good. Please don't. We have a plan." I explained about the truth spell. "Once you locate her though, can you call me?"

"I was about to say that Don Dunfield from Palm Ridge just called. His men located her rental car at a local motel. He is awaiting my instructions."

I motioned for a piece of paper and pencil. "What's the name of the motel?"

He told me. "But Glinda, we have to bring her in for

questioning at some point."

"I totally agree. I have a plan—or at least I will have one shortly. I'll call you back when it is fully flushed out. It will involve you and Steve."

"It's another Glinda Goodall special, I take it?"

I chuckled at that nickname. "It is."

"No problem then. I'll let Don know to stand by."

Nash was the best. "Thank you."

"Just make sure we get enough proof to convict her."

People sure did expect a lot. "No problem."

Once he hung up, I told my partners in crime that one issue was solved. "Next we need to convince Jude to help."

"I don't think that will be a problem," Jaxson said.

"Let's hope."

I called him, and Jude answered on the first ring. "Yes?"

He must still be wondering how he didn't recognize that Francine had become unhinged. "This is Glinda. I was wondering if you'd be willing to help us find evidence against Francine?" I held my breath, hoping he hadn't changed his mind about her guilt.

"Tell me where and when, and I'll be there."

Now there was a good man. "Can you come to our office? We have a plan." Or at least part of a plan.

"I'll be there in five."

I turned to Jaxson and Rihanna. "Any ideas how this is going to work?"

SHERIFF DUNFIELD HAD provided us with the location of

Francine's hotel. Furthermore, his men were there waiting for us. Should anything go wrong, they'd intercede.

Jude pulled into the hotel parking lot. "You know what to say?" I asked.

"Yes. I just hope she buys it."

I reached out and squeezed his arm. "She wants to. I think she'll believe you, because she needs to believe you, if that makes sense."

"Not really, but we need to give it a try."

I was there to add credibility to the story that someone wanted her dead.

Jude knocked on the hotel door. "It's me, Francine. It's Jude. It's really important I talk with you."

I swear it took thirty seconds before she answered. Was she scared? Or didn't she trust Jude?

When Francine opened up and saw me, her slight cheer disappeared. She stood up straighter, acting as if she needed to appear strong. "What's going on?"

"Can we come in?" Jude asked. "I don't want anyone to see you."

"Sure." She turned to me. "Why are you here?"

That wasn't nice. "I've recently learned that someone is out to kill you."

It looked like she pretended to stumble, probably so that Jude would rush to help her, which he did. I had to say he was playing his part well.

"Sit down, Francine," he said. "We're here to help you."

She sat on the bed while Jude and I used the two chairs at the tiny table. "Who is trying to kill me?"

I wanted to stick to the truth the best I could, only I

didn't know who the culprit was. I needed a name she'd believe, and the only reasonable one was Patricia Diaz Haltern. "Patricia."

"Patricia? Kyle's old girlfriend?" I nodded. "Why?"

"I couldn't say. It's not because you and Kyle can be together anymore. I'm sure she knows he is dead."

"How do you know she wants to kill me?"

If she believed this part, I think we might convince her to come with us. "Patricia contacted Andorra Leyton to put a lethal spell on you." If I'd told her it was really Elizabeth, she might not believe me since only Andorra knew Kyle.

"Andorra? Why would she agree?"

"Patricia and Andorra were good friends in high school. Patricia knows that Andorra is a witch. As am I."

She chuckled. "A witch? Do you fly around on a broom?"

Like I hadn't heard that before. If she was trying to make us think she wasn't a member of the occult, she'd have to do better than that. "Hardly. We do spells. And right now, Patricia has asked Andorra to kill you."

She laughed, but it was filled with some fear. "Why are you telling me this?" She turned to Jude. "Why are you really here?"

"We have a lot to talk about. For starters, I want to apologize." He turned to me. "Can you give me a few minutes alone with Francine?"

"Sure." We figured he might have to use his charms to convince her that he had her best interests at heart.

I stepped outside. Even after I did a quick perusal of the parking lot, I didn't see anyone who looked like an officer of the law, but I had to trust someone was there.

I walked back to the car and leaned against it. As much as I wanted to call or text Jaxson or Andorra, I didn't dare. I couldn't chance Francine watching me. She might think it was a setup—which it was.

By the time the hotel door opened, my nerves were raw. If Jude didn't succeed in convincing Francine to go with us, I'm not sure what our next step would be. Even if Steve brought her in for questioning, they had no proof to hold her.

To my delight, Jude was escorting Francine out of her room. She didn't have anything with her other than her purse, which meant she wasn't planning to run. I let out a slow breath.

I could only hope the rest of the plan went as smoothly. It involved several things going right, and with my track record, who knows how it would turn out.

As soon as Francine reached me, she grabbed my arm, and I tried to keep a neutral face.

"Jude explained everything. I can't thank you enough for helping me."

"I'm happy to." Just not in the same way she expected. We climbed into the car. I sat in back and let the *lovebirds* be in front. "Did Jude explain what has to happen next?"

"Not really. He's not a witchy person. He said he didn't really understand."

That was smart to pass the buck. "Elizabeth, Andorra's cousin, was able to find out what spell Andorra planned to use on you. There is a blocking spell that Elizabeth wants to put on you in case she tries it."

"Why again did Andorra agree to kill me? She doesn't know me. I thought she was Kyle's friend."

"She is, which was why Patricia—who has no witch powers—is forcing Andorra to do her bidding. If Andorra doesn't do as Patricia asks, Patricia will kill Elizabeth, their grandmother, and eventually Andorra."

Francine appeared shaken. "I had no idea."

That's because none of it was true. It then occurred to me that if Patricia—or whoever this caller turned out to be—had the guts to harm Elizabeth and their grandmother, why not just kill Francine herself? Did she think she'd be considered a person of interest? No matter how hard I tried, I couldn't figure it out. I was missing something. I had to be.

During the rest of the trip back to Witch's Cove, Francine sort of flirted with Jude. I had to give him an acting award since he appeared to be interested in her—at least, I hoped it was an act. I couldn't wait to find out what he'd told her in the hotel room to smooth things over between them.

None too soon, we arrived at the Hex and Bones store, which was closed, of course, since it was rather late. At the front door, I knocked, and Elizabeth answered. Andorra was supposed to be out of sight as was Drake since he had no reason to be there.

"It's back here. I have everything set up. Once I do the incantation, if Andorra tries to put a curse on you, it won't work."

"I've never heard of anything like that." Francine sounded sincere.

I expected her to say that. "Why would you know? You aren't a witch." I knew she wouldn't dare deny it.

"No, so what's going to happen to Andorra when Patricia finds out that I'm not dead?"

"Don't worry. Jude, along with Drake and Jaxson have promised to protect her until we can figure out how to catch the perpetrator." In truth, a powerful witch could probably kill Andorra even with two bodyguards.

"Again, thank you."

Elizabeth led us into the dimly lit storage room. There was a curtain to the side that I suspected concealed a few people. In the middle of the room sat a table.

"I am so sorry this Patricia lady threatened my family and your well-being," Elizabeth said.

"Where is Andorra?" Francine asked.

"With Drake somewhere. She has no idea we are doing this. I know she wouldn't approve since she values my life, but I can't in all good conscience allow another life to be taken because of jealousy or whatever is at play. Please have a seat so I may begin."

Francine sat down. I nodded to Jude to move to the back of the room. We needed space to conduct the truth spell. Off to the side sat Hugo in his gargoyle form. Andorra assured us that he would come through when needed.

"Ready?" I asked.

"Yes."

I looked over at Hugo and mentally willed him to change into his human form. As if he understood the severity of the situation, he silently transformed into a person. Yes!! I'd told Jude that this would happen, but no one can really be prepared for when it did. He sucked in a very audible breath. Just as Francine turned around, Hugo was instantly behind her. He pressed his hands to her shoulders, and she immediately faced forward again.

From what Andorra had told us, Hugo had the ability to bend people to his will. We still needed to do the truth spell, but now Francine didn't have the will to complain.

Like a well-choreographed dance, Andorra and Rihanna emerged from behind the curtain, and I rushed to the table. The four of us picked up a candle and encircled Francine. It was similar to what I'd seen Levy and his coven do when they had to remove the power from an evil warlock.

In this case, our job was merely to get Francine to confess. Even though Elizabeth found this spell, I conferred with Levy to make sure we weren't missing something. If all went well, we'd get her to tell us everything.

Elizabeth lit the bowl of herbs, and a red smoke rose upward. I'd never seen that color before, but then, I'd never participated in this kind of spell either. Rihanna handed us a piece of paper with the spell written on it since we hadn't had time to memorize it. In unison, we said the four-lines in a slow, measured manner. I wasn't sure what would happen when we finished, but apparently, Elizabeth did.

She pulled out another piece of paper. "Francine Xavier, did you kill Kyle Covington?"

Before Francine had a chance to answer, Jaxson parted the curtain and aimed the camera at her. His role was to record her confession. Steve came through the door and quietly moved behind Francine. Nash was assigned to guard the front of the building in case something went wrong.

"Yes," she intoned.

Oh, my goodness. It worked!! Even though she was answering under the influence of a spell, a jury would never know that.

"How did you kill him?"

"I placed some herbs in the bottles used to make the punch."

"Weren't you worried others might drink from the bowl before Kyle?" Elizabeth asked.

I had to admit that Steve's questions were good ones.

"As soon as those girls mixed it, I said a spell to combine them so the ingredients wouldn't float to the surface. I then did a second spell that only affected Kyle's glass."

"In other words, you poisoned Kyle, meaning for him to die, right?" That came from Elizabeth improvising. Good for her. The jury wouldn't care about a spell, only the intent to do harm.

"Yes."

That should be enough to send Francine away. I stepped into her view. "Why? Why did you do it?"

"He'd often spoken of the girl he left behind when he went to college. I knew when he told me he wanted to delay the wedding that he planned to leave me if she was willing to give him a second chance."

I had to assume she was referring to Patricia. Steve said he hadn't found any messages between the two on either phone. Was this all in Francine's head?

Jude touched my arm, and I jumped. He held up one finger to indicate he wanted to ask her something. I nodded. Of all of us, he needed closure the most.

"Francine, did you mean what you said when you claimed you loved me?"

Her laugh scared even me. "No."

"Then why did you say it?" Jude seemed hurt.

"I can't spend the rest of my life working. You and Kyle had so much money. I just needed one of you to share some with me."

Wow. That was cold. Real cold. Steve held up a hand and moved behind Francine. Andorra nodded at Hugo who then stepped in front of Francine, placed a hand on her shoulder, causing her to jerk.

Eyes wide, she looked around. "What's going on?"

"Francine Xavier," Steve said. "You are under arrest for the murder of Kyle Covington."

Chapter Sixteen

FRANCINE LAUGHED. "YOU have to be kidding. I did not kill Kyle."

"That's not what you just told us," Steve said as he helped her to her feet and cuffed her.

Jaxson continued recording. When I looked for Hugo, he'd retreated into his statue form. All I could say was that Andorra's familiar was one creepy dude. I was glad that Iggy hadn't been here. He might have interfered, begging Hugo to return to his human form once more. I would have to let him visit at some point.

Francine continued to argue as Steve led her out. "I'll send Nash in for the camera," he said.

"You bet."

I blew out my candle, and then Andorra flipped on the lights. "Okay, that was intense, people."

Jude cleared his throat. Darn. I'd almost forgotten about him. He must be reeling from everything. Drake and Andorra helped Elizabeth straighten up as I went over to Jude.

"How are you doing?" I asked.

"How do you think? I never even knew witchcraft existed before Kyle died. In a few days' time, I've seen a statue turn into a person, and then four women holding candles saying some words that made Francine admit that she killed Kyle. It was insane."

"I can understand how bizarre and strange it seems. I do have one favor to ask."

"Name it—assuming you don't ask me to try my hand at witchcraft."

I inwardly smiled. That wasn't how witchcraft worked. I placed a hand on his arm. "Can you take a day or two to process this and not discuss it with anyone until we figure out who wanted to kill Francine?"

He huffed out a laugh. "No problem. Who would I tell anyway? It's not like anyone would believe me. And I certainly don't need my clients demanding that I be institutionalized."

I rubbed his arm. "I'm really sorry."

He nodded. "Right now, I need to figure out how to deal with losing Kyle."

"I doubt it is important at this point, but do you know who Kyle left his money to?" I asked.

"Yes. Some would have gone to Francine, though he never told her that. He loved her, but he must have sensed something was off. I figured that was why he wanted to delay the wedding."

"What about the rest of his millions?" My information could have been wrong about how wealthy he really was.

"I get his portion of the company, and his parents inherit the earnings from his investments, now that Francine will be in jail."

"Thank you for all of your help. Again, I am sorry for your loss." I looked over my shoulder at Jaxson and the gang who seemed to have finished their chores. "Hey, we'll probably go to the Tiki Hut Grill for a drink. Do you want to join us, Jude?"

He shook his head. "I hope you don't mind, but I need to spend some alone time. I might stop over tomorrow to see if you need me to help with anything else."

"Thanks." Jude was a great guy. Or was he?

After we locked up the store, Elizabeth and Andorra declined our offer of a drink. Drake gently clasped Andorra's arm. "We should all stick together, or at least be in public for a while. Don't forget, the person who asked Elizabeth to do the spell on Francine is still out there."

Elizabeth's shoulders sagged. "I can't live like this."

"I know," I said. "We need to come up with another plan to find this person and take them down. Come on. You can order a soda at the restaurant."

Elizabeth nodded. "Okay."

We all headed over to the Tiki Hut Grill. I would have suggested we sit outside, but it was a bit too chilly for me. Besides, being inside provided us with more privacy, which was one reason why I didn't want to go to the diner. The booths were too close to each other.

A server I'd never seen before came over and took our order. I caved and asked for some nachos and dip since this whole spell thing took a lot out of me. "I want to thank everyone for doing such a great job," I said.

Elizabeth almost gave us a full smile. "It was kind of amazing. I've never done a spell with a group before. Our energies combined to create a powerful force."

"I agree. I could almost feel the power surge inside of me," I said.

"Me, too," Andorra chimed in.

"I'm no lawyer, but it seems to me that Francine's taped confession should be good enough to convict her," Drake said.

"If not in a regular court, she'll go down in a court of her peers," Jaxson said.

"Did your friend Levy get back to you about the spell Francine used in the gym?" Andorra asked.

"Not yet. Even if they don't find anything, we should have enough to convict her. If they locate the spell, it will be the *icing on the cake*, should we need to go the peer-review court way."

Our server returned with our drinks and snacks and then left. I raised my glass. "I realize that we'd all like to go home and rest, but the funeral is almost here, and I fear that whoever is behind this mess will slip out of our fingers if we don't figure something out."

"I agree," Jaxson said, "but we have no leads."

I waited for someone to make a suggestion, but there was no obvious choice. "Let's list who might be involved. I'm thinking the same people who we believed might have killed Kyle would be suspects for trying to kill Francine."

Drake shook his head. "Just the opposite."

"What do you mean?" I asked.

"Answer this question: Who would want Francine dead?"

"Drake's right," Andorra said. "Elizabeth was approached after Kyle had been killed. They want justice for Kyle's death."

"I like the vigilante approach. Another witch might know we can never prove for sure that Francine was guilty. After all, the only evidence is her mumbling something a few seconds before Kyle died. No jury would believe spells are real anyway." This was really depressing.

Jaxson sipped his drink. "Let's list who would want to avenge Kyle's death."

"Jude, but he's not a warlock," I said.

"Patricia," Elizabeth added. "Do you know for sure if she is or isn't a witch?"

"Andorra was closer to her than anyone," I said.

"I don't believe she is, but it's possible she hid it from me in high school. I kind of doubt it, though, since I told her I practiced the art of magic, and she seemed surprised."

"That could eliminate her," I said. "Especially since she gave Steve and Nash the video of Francine doing the spell. By helping the police focus their attention on the killer, she might believe justice had been served. Unless we are way off base, there were only two people left. One is Ronnie Taggert and the other is Christian Durango."

Andorra grabbed some nachos and munched on them. "Ronnie might want to send Francine a present for killing the man who refused to bail him out not harm her."

She had a point. "With Kyle dead, I don't see him caring if anyone was caught."

"Remember, Christian is a warlock—make that an angry warlock," Andorra said.

I didn't see her logic. "So? If he needed a spell put on Francine, he would have done it himself. Why would he call Elizabeth and ask her? That would only add another person to the mix, increasing the chance of him being caught."

The group sat there for a bit, clearly stumped.

"We should look at Jude again?" Drake asked.

I really liked the guy, but maybe I was being blinded by

his grief. "Rihanna was certain he was genuinely distraught over Kyle's death, so it makes sense that he might want revenge against the killer. He admitted Francine was angry about the wedding delay, but did he know she had it in her to kill Kyle?"

"If Francine figured out she was to inherit some of Kyle's fortune, she might want to kill Jude next to give her a larger portion of the pie. Jude could have suspected this and decided to take her out first." This was getting way too complicated.

Jaxson whistled. "When did you become so cynical?"

My mouth opened. "It's not cynicism when I use logic. Right?"

Everyone chuckled.

We spent the rest of the evening chatting about everything other than Francine and Kyle. As hard as it was for me, I needed the mental space. Too bad, I didn't have any brainstorming ideas—only a sense of doom.

Since the person who'd threatened Elizabeth and her family was still out there, she and Andorra planned to spend the night with Drake. For that I was grateful. I might have asked Jaxson to take his usual place on my couch, but I hadn't been threatened in any way.

After we settled up with the bill, everyone dispersed. Jaxson walked me upstairs, gave me a very sensual kiss goodnight and then left after promising to keep his thinking cap on.

THE NEXT MORNING, I stopped over at the sheriff's

department and managed to convince Steve to ask a few key people to stay in town until a day after the funeral. I had no idea how I thought one day would be enough to figure things out, but I'd take any extension I could get.

I'd just arrived at our office when Levy called. "Hey," I said.

"I heard congrats are in order."

"Thanks. Did you learn anything about the spell?"

"I did, and I already emailed it to you."

He was efficient. "I just walked into work. What's the short of it?"

"It is a very specific and powerful spell. You need to beware of Francine. She is a powerful witch."

"She's in custody. You don't think either Nash or Steve are in jeopardy, do you?"

"No. Just don't let her get her hands on any herbs."

No chance of that. "I appreciate all of your speedy hard work."

"Anytime," he said.

I disconnected, set my bag with Iggy inside on the table, and went over to Jaxson. I pulled up a chair and sat next to him. I then told him about Levy's call. "Let me send the spell to Steve. I'm not sure how it can help, though."

"If Francine is tried in her court of peers, it might."

"You're right." I forwarded it with a brief message. I then returned my attention to Jaxson. "Any brainstorming ideas last night?"

"Not yet."

"We have to do something to find this mysterious caller."

He faced me. "I'd like nothing more. Give me some

suggestions."

I was out of them, but that wasn't going to stop me. As if Kyle was looking down on us, my phone rang. "Again?" When I looked at the caller ID, I tensed. "It's Rihanna. She should be in school." I swiped the phone. "Hey."

"You won't believe this." Her excitement had me sitting up straighter. Rihanna never called from school. This must be good. "What is it?"

"Yesterday, Lena went to get her oil changed."

I wasn't sure how to respond to that less than exciting news. "Okay."

"You don't understand. She took her car to the garage where Casi's brother, Christian, works."

Was she going to tell me they are now dating or something? The age difference would be rather significant. "And?"

"No one was out front, so she walked into the shop. She stopped when she saw a woman hand Christian a big wad of cash."

"Maybe the repair job was extensive." I had no idea why she was telling me this.

"No. She heard this woman say that she was not at all happy that Andorra didn't stay where she was supposed to for more than a few hours. Christian then called this woman by name. He said Patricia, as in Patricia Haltern."

My cousin had my full attention. "Wow. Was Lena certain Patricia said Andorra's name?"

"Yes."

"Hold on." I put the call on speaker. "Christian is a warlock. Are you saying that Patricia paid Christian to put a spell on Andorra so that she'd drive to a restaurant parking lot?"

"He didn't say where."

I had to picture all of this in my mind. "Do you think that Lena was accurate in what she saw?"

"Totally. Want to know why?"

Chapter Seventeen

RIHANNA UNDERSTOOD THAT I disliked guessing games. "Yes, please."

"Lena kind of has a crush on Casi's brother. So, get this. She videotaped him. I think she was jealous that he was with a woman."

"She taped him? Can you hear what was said?"

"Yes."

Jaxson leaned forward. "Can you send the video to us?"

"It will be in your inbox in a moment." Just then Jaxson's email pinged.

That was impressive. "Please thank Lena for us. She might have helped solve a very important case."

"I will." A rather shrill bell rang in the background. "Gotta get to class."

"Have fun." As soon as I disconnected, Jaxson downloaded the video. Together we watched it. "Turn it up," I said.

At the end of the short interchange, Christian faced Patricia. "And Francine? Did you get what you wanted, whatever that was?"

"Not yet, but I will. I have that covered though."

Christian waved the wad of cash. "Thanks for this. It was the easiest money I've ever earned."

Patricia nodded, turned around, and left. There was no doubt that Patricia was involved in wanting Francine dead. "We have to show Steve this."

"What can he do with it? It's more witch mumbo jumbo. Andorra wasn't harmed, and Francine is alive."

He was right. "I somehow get the sense that Christian wasn't totally sure of the purpose of the spell."

"I don't think Patricia specifically called it a spell."

"Maybe not, but it was clear Christian was to convince Andorra to go to some restaurant and wait there."

Jaxson pushed back his chair and grabbed his phone. "That might be. In any case, I'll email this to Steve. Then we can go over there. We might be missing something, but if nothing else, he should keep an eye on Patricia."

I turned to Iggy. "Do you want to come?"

"Why?" He dropped down onto his stomach and lowered his head.

That didn't look good. "Are you missing Hugo?"

"Maybe."

"When this is over, I'll ask Andorra to see if maybe he'll return to his human form for you." I didn't want to promise anything since I had no idea how Hugo really worked.

"Okay, but why do you want me to go to the sheriff's office."

I shrugged. "Maybe to prove that Francine really is a witch."

"You know she is. You saw her do the spell, and you said she admitted that she killed Kyle."

"I know, but it's nice to be sure. Besides, we need to do some brainstorming, and we can always use the ideas from the great detective Iggy Goodall."

He lifted his upper body. "Really?"

"Really." It was easy to please him. I placed him in my purse, and then Jaxson and I headed over to see Steve. If the funeral hadn't already been scheduled, I would have waited for Rihanna to get back from school, but time was of the essence.

Once we chatted with Pearl for a bit, we found Steve in his office. He was watching the video and motioned we take a seat. When he finished, he leaned back in his chair. "I can see that Patricia paid Christian to do some work for her."

I figured he was going to say that the work could have been for a car repair. "Yes, but he mentions Andorra by name."

"True, but Patricia might have needed a car part from him. I think this has potential, but any lawyer would tear it apart. It's not specific enough."

Darn it. That was disappointing. "Is there anything we can do?"

Iggy crawled out of my purse. Steve's eyes opened for a moment. "Hello, fellow."

Iggy looked at me. "Why does he talk to me when he knows he can't understand the answer?"

"He's being nice."

"Whatever."

I blew out a breath. "What are we going to do?" I asked Steve.

"Do? What do you mean?" Steve asked.

As if he didn't know. "While Elizabeth and Andorra are with Drake until this mess is resolved, Patricia may not stop until Francine is dead."

"Francine is safe here."

"That's not the point. We need to find a way to catch Patricia in the act of trying to get her revenge. She might try to enlist another witch and threaten Elizabeth and her family."

Steve crossed his arms. "How do you propose to catch Patricia—or prove she is the guilty party?"

Iggy piped up. "I know."

I looked down at him. "You know? Tell me, oh wise one."

"If Patricia believed that Francine was dead, she'd have no need to harm Elizabeth or Andorra."

I relayed to Steve what Iggy said. "That won't prove Patricia is guilty though. She didn't kill anyone or harm anyone—yet," he said.

"Isn't hiring someone to kidnap someone wrong?" I held up a hand. "Kidnap isn't the right word, I know."

Jaxson placed a hand on my arm. "More like mind controlled."

I leaned back. "We should hire Christian to do the same to Patricia. See how she likes it, and yes, I'm only kidding."

"You're the witch. Can't you pull a rabbit out of your hat and come up with something special?" Steve asked.

He'd been watching too many television shows.

"I wish. What we need is for Patricia to call Elizabeth again and say her time is up. Then Elizabeth can claim that Francine is now dead and to leave her family alone."

"Great, but Patricia will want proof," Steve said.

"Then we'll give her proof." Just as soon as I figure out how to do that. "But first, we need to prove the caller is Patricia. We can put a trace on Elizabeth's phone, right?"

"If I have Elizabeth's permission, I can tap her phone, yes, but until Patricia stays on the line long enough, we won't be able to trace it back to her."

Iggy lifted a leg. It kind of looked as if he was raising his hand. How polite of him. "Do you have something to say?"

"Yes. How about if when this weirdo caller contacts Elizabeth, she tells the caller that Francine is dead and in the morgue? You can catch her that way."

I chuckled. "And when Patricia shows up, we can assume she is guilty?"

Iggy scratched his head. "My brain hurts."

My brain hurt, too. I told Steve Iggy's solution.

"It has potential. The only person who would have heard that Francine is dead would be this caller."

"Yes, and if Patricia goes to the morgue, she'd have to specifically ask to see Francine." Jaxson said.

"I can have Elissa wear a wire," Steve said. "The sound from that lab camera isn't always clear."

He'd had the need to look at if before? Interesting.

"Then what?" Jaxson asked.

"Here's a crazy idea that just might work," I said. "A long time ago, Bertha told me about some group of witches who made one person look like another. It didn't last long, but it could be enough to fool Patricia."

"Suppose you can do that," Jaxson said. "It's really hard to look dead. Not breathing for a while might be impossible to pull off."

"No. I didn't explain it well enough. We'll start with a dead person and make that person look like Francine—not with makeup but with magic." I looked up at Steve. "The catch is that Francine would have to agree to go along with this. It's painless, I promise." Or I hoped it was.

"I imagine she'll want to get back at the person who pointed the finger at her," he said.

"Yes, and you could even say you'd speak to the attorney on her behalf if she cooperates."

"That might work." Steve sounded impressed.

"Where are you going to get this dead person?" Jaxson asked.

"I imagine Elissa can call around and borrow a body for our little sting operation."

Steve tapped his pencil against his yellow pad. "How do you get Patricia to call Elizabeth in the first place. She has to know that kidnapping Andorra didn't scare Elizabeth. Maybe she'll give up."

Iggy looked up. "Ask Christian to help."

"Why would he do that? No one admits to a crime."

"What did Iggy say?" Steve asked.

I told him. "Christian has been in and out of trouble since high school."

Jaxson cleared his throat. "Sounds like someone else I know. This might give him a chance to do some good for a change."

My boyfriend was talking about himself. "Could be. Steve, can you offer him immunity? I really don't think Christian knew why he was bending Andorra's mind to his will."

"That's up to the district attorney, but I'm betting he'd be willing to deal. I'll call Nash and have him pick Christian up."

Yikes. This little operation might go down. "Ask Christian to then call Patricia and tell her he heard that Francine was dead, assuming Francine agrees to this."

He nodded. "Can do."

"In the meantime, I need Elizabeth to contact her grand-mother and ask about that spell." I crossed my fingers for good luck, though I don't remember that superstition ever actually working.

"What time would you like to have Christian call Patricia and tell her the good news?"

"Give me an hour. I need to fill Elizabeth and Andorra in on my plan since I need their help. Once Rihanna returns from school, we'll have enough witch power to do this."

"I'll be in touch. And thank you again."

As soon as we left, Jaxson and I rushed over to the Hex and Bones Apothecary. Drake, and hopefully Hugo, would be there protecting the ladies, while Trace, one of Drake's assistants would be managing the wine and cheese store.

When I stepped inside, I was relieved to see Elizabeth helping a customer and Andorra chatting with Drake.

"Is Hugo here?" Iggy asked.

"Let's see." I didn't want to freak out the customer, so I waved to Andorra and slipped behind the counter to check the back room. To my delight, Hugo was standing in his spot. I lifted Iggy out and placed him near his new friend. "You're welcome to discuss our plan. Hugo might have some suggestions."

Iggy didn't answer. Instead, he waddled over to Hugo who picked him up. Happy that my familiar was in good hands, I returned to the outer room and went over to Drake and Andorra.

Apparently, Jaxson had just filled them in.

Andorra smiled. "I think the plan is outstanding. I'll call Memaw right now. She'll be returning to Witch's Cove in a few days, and I can't wait to have her here."

I was thrilled too. "Great."

Andorra stepped into the back room and made her call. It probably wouldn't do the business any good if a customer learned we were using magic in this rather strange manner.

"Do you think this can work?" Drake asked.

"If Christian cooperates, and Francine is willing to help, and if we can locate the spell in time, as well as a spare body, sure, it can work." Who was I kidding?

Jaxson rubbed my arm. "Don't stress out. You can do this."

"The funeral is tomorrow. We'll also need Elissa to have a body delivered to the morgue by five, assuming Patricia believes Christian when he tells her that Francine is dead."

Drake nodded. "Who's to say she'd even want proof?"

"I wish I knew her better to know how she'd react. There are so many moving parts that it scares me."

When Jaxson wrapped me in his arms, the tension in my body disappeared. I had no intention of moving. Ever. I wouldn't have either if four tiny feet hadn't crawled up my leg.

I stepped out of Jaxson's embrace and lifted Iggy up. "What's up?"

"Hugo had a good idea."

"I'm always up for ideas. What does he suggest?"

"He said that if Christian asks Patricia to meet him, I can be there and put the trance on Patricia to convince her to go to the morgue. It's the same spell that Christian put on

Andorra."

Iggy had never performed a spell, so I wasn't sure he could do it, and right now might not be the best time to test it out. Too much was at stake. "You and Hugo are brilliant, but how about if we ask Christian to do it instead?"

Iggy scratched his face. "I guess that would work, but only because we don't have a lot of time for me to practice."

I lifted Iggy to my lips and kissed him, happy that he understood. "You are really smart. Let me suggest that to Steve."

"What just happened?" Drake asked.

"Jaxson, can you fill in your brother while I make the call?"

"Can do."

I stepped outside since Andorra was still in the back room. I called Steve and explained the plan. "If Christian can't or won't do it, then let me know, and I'll try the spell. If he agrees, tell him we'll owe him one."

Steve chuckled. "I'm not sure that is how the law works, but I think I can convince him."

"If you need some leverage, remember that Casi and Rihanna are really good friends. He doesn't want to wreck it for his sister, right?"

"I got this. I will call you later. Christian will be here momentarily."

Showtime.

Chapter Eighteen

"I STILL CAN'T believe both Christian and Francine agreed to do this," I said. Steve had just called back and said everything was a go.

"Are we sure Patricia will go to the morgue at six?" Jaxson asked.

"Christian said he had it under control. I honestly don't want to know what he'll have to do to get her there. If it's a spell, fine. If he has to make up some excuse and escort Patricia there, that's okay, too."

"What's next?" Drake asked.

Before I could answer, Rihanna rushed into the Hex and Bones. I'd texted her and asked if she could come there straight from school. She needed to learn the spell, as did the others.

I had contacted our medical examiner, who said an elderly woman had passed away this morning. I wasn't sure whether age made a difference, but she would have to do.

"Hey," Rihanna said. "Have you all started?"

"Nope. We were waiting for you."

Elizabeth poked her head out of the back room. "Can everyone come in here, please?"

I hoped that meant she had learned of a transforming

spell, something I'd never attempted, probably because I'd heard it took multiple witches to conduct the spell.

"We need to close early," Andorra said.

Elizabeth nodded. "We will. The spell will only take about two minutes to perform."

"How long will it last? We don't want Patricia to arrive late and our elderly woman turns back to her old self."

"That would be terrible. The book says it lasts about forty-five minutes."

"That doesn't give us a big window. Is it possible to repeat the spell if need be?" I didn't imagine the spell would require a lot of ingredients.

"I didn't ask Memaw, but I'll take extra herbs just in case," Andorra said.

She walked over to the printer and grabbed the spell and gave a copy to Rihanna and Elizabeth.

"Did Steve say what time Christian planned to have Patricia arrive?" Rihanna asked.

"The plan is for six, but we should be ready by quarter of."

Jaxson checked his phone. "It's five now. Can you ladies take care of the spell stuff while Glinda and I make sure everything is good to go at the morgue?" Andorra and Elizabeth nodded.

"I'll watch them," Iggy said.

"Thanks. I'd ask you to come, but I know you don't like the smell of dead bodies."

He lifted up. "Like you do?"

No one did, but after a while you got used to it. That was the hazard of having funeral directors as parents. Knowing that the spell was in good hands, and that Steve would be handling the transfer of Francine to the medical examiner's office, Jaxson and I headed over there. I wanted to check things out to make sure we hadn't forgotten anything.

When we arrived, Gavin answered the door and led us back to where his mother was setting things up. I'd asked her to have a second table available where Francine could recline. She needed to be near the body in order for the transformation to occur. To say I was nervous was an understatement.

"Glinda, Jaxson. I have to say I'm intrigued by this, but can you assure me that the woman's body will return to its current state? The family has requested an autopsy, and I want to make sure it's the correct body."

"I believe so. It should last no more than forty-five minutes."

"Good. What do you need me to do?"

I went over the questions she needed to ask. "Remember, should anything happen, Steve is right outside. You gave him access to the video feed, right?"

"Yes. Nash told me he'd be around, too."

Of course, he would. The men around here were highly protective of their women.

After Jaxson helped Gavin carry in another table and set it up next to the dead woman, I called Drake. I didn't want to bother the other ladies since they would be practicing the spell.

My cell chimed a few minutes later. I checked it. "They're ready. They'll be here shortly."

"I'll let them in," Gavin said. He turned around and headed to the front.

He was such a good kid. I was so happy that Rihanna and Gavin had found each other. Five minutes later, Gavin escorted Drake, Rihanna, Elizabeth, and Andorra into the morgue. Both Elizabeth and Andorra held a hand over their noses. Rihanna was probably getting used to the smell, and while I was sure it was grossing Drake out, he pretended as if it was cool.

The plan was that once the dead woman looked like Francine, we'd all leave. I would have loved to stay and watch Patricia's reaction at seeing the deceased look like Francine, but unfortunately, there was no place to hide in this room. We'd have to be content to watch the replay.

Andorra nudged me. "Oh, sorry. Where should I set up?"

Elissa, Jaxson, and I had placed a small table for her in the corner. "Over there," I said.

It didn't take her long to get ready. Andorra then passed out the papers with the spell to her cousin and Rihanna. My job was to pass my crystal over Francine from toe to head and then move over to the dead body. When I reached her, they would begin the chant. I guess it was kind of like scanning an object and then uploading it into a 3-D printer. Having never attempted this before, I really wasn't sure if it was going to work.

Elizabeth assured me that the book gave specific instructions that my stone had to be used. It might be why the spell hadn't been performed very often. The need to find three witches and a fourth with a magic stone was a tall order.

Rihanna looked over at me. "You got this, Glinda."

I would forgive her for reading my mind this time. As I tried to calm myself, the door to the morgue clicked open.

Here goes.

Steve escorted Francine into the room. She checked out each of us but said nothing. I don't know what I thought she'd do. Apologize for killing a person we cared about? Say she hoped we were successful so that Patricia would get her just due?

"Where do you want her?" Steve asked.

"Francine, you can lie down on the table," Elissa instructed.

She glanced over at the sheeted body to her right. "Do I need to undress or anything?"

"No," Andorra piped up.

Since she'd spoken with her grandmother, I had to defer to her. Patricia was expected to arrive in fifteen-minutes—assuming Christian did as he promised—which meant we needed to begin. Andorra turned off the overhead lights but kept some task lights on. Then they lit candles.

Elissa covered Francine with a sheet up to her neck. I wasn't sure why, other than it was cold in the room.

"Glinda, you may begin." Elizabeth sounded very much in control, and that made me feel better.

After removing my necklace, I swung the stone back and forth from Francine's feet, across her body, and up to her neck. Since the face was the most important part of this spell, I spent more time *scanning* it.

When I finished, I looked up and nodded. All three began the spell. They would keep repeating it until I'd finished with my part. Even though I didn't care about this dead woman's lower body changing, I wanted to follow protocol. I began at her feet, swinging my pendant upward until I reached her neck. I had no idea what would happen, but it wasn't what did.

As I was swinging my pink diamond between her eyes, the gem suddenly started to glow. My heart squeezed tight. I waited for a chill to cross my body that signaled my grandmother had come into her ghostly form—or this dead woman had—but after briefly looking around and not seeing any ghost, I continued. Just as the stone passed over the woman's forehead, her whole face changed.

"Glinda?" Jaxson stepped behind me and clasped my shoulders.

I'd frozen. This dead woman looked exactly like Francine. The transformation stunned me into near paralysis, but Jaxson's warm hands soon brought me back to reality. The stone then returned to its normal state. "I did it. Or, rather, we did it."

"Yes." He nodded to Elissa, who turned on the overhead lights, nearly blinding me.

Steve helped Francine up. "It's okay to leave, right?" he asked.

He never was one to question things, but perhaps he thought if she left, something might happen to the dead woman.

Elizabeth answered. "Yes."

The two of them hurried out. I had no idea how long we'd been in the room. The last thing we needed was for Patricia to see any of us leaving the morgue. "We need to go, too."

Elissa folded up the sheet that had been covering Francine. "Don't worry. I've shown bodies to loved ones before."

I wasn't worried about her. It was the body returning to her former self that troubled me. "Text me if something goes wrong, though I'm not really sure what we can do once Patricia arrives."

"It will be fine. Go."

We all left. Steve and Francine would be waiting in his squad car down the street until after Patricia left the morgue. If she failed to give away any of her involvement in Francine's death, Steve and the very much alive Francine would show up. Naturally, Steve would be wired to record that interaction.

Nash would be hiding along the side of the building to take photos of Patricia. It was possible that Christian would have to come with her to make it seem legit.

Drake suggested we head on over to the ice cream shop to celebrate, but I was too nervous. "I need to retrieve Iggy. You guys can go ahead if you want."

Andorra placed a hand on my shoulder. "No. We are in this together. We'll go back to the Hex and Bones with you. If by some chance Patricia comes looking for me or Elizabeth, we'll be where we're supposed to be."

That made sense. We all drove back, and once we arrived, Elizabeth flipped the closed sign to open.

I kept checking the time. "Patricia should be at the morgue by now."

No surprise, Jaxson stepped behind me and drew my back to his chest. "You and the girls have done everything possible. It's up to fate to do the rest. If Patricia is guilty, she'll slip up."

"Let's hope."

"If she seems happy that Francine is dead, what kind of time will she get?" Rihanna asked.

I shrugged. "I don't know. She did blackmail Elizabeth into killing someone for her. I haven't researched it, but that's a crime in my book."

"Mine, too."

Drake stepped next to Andorra. "Look at the bright side. If Patricia is convinced that Francine is dead, and Steve feels he doesn't have enough evidence to prosecute, she'll go home and leave everyone alone. If he has proof, then she'll do time."

Drake always was the super logical one. "I like it," Andorra said.

When I entered the back room to get Iggy, he was pacing. "About time you got here."

I looked around for Hugo and finally located his statue in a different spot. "Did Hugo say why he transformed to his stone self?"

"Andorra isn't in danger anymore and neither is Elizabeth."

"Good to know." I bent down and picked him up. "Did you and Hugo have a chance to bond?"

"I did. I wish I had more powers."

"You have plenty. You can cloak yourself. That's more power than ninety-nine percent of the people in the world."

He lifted his chest. "Yeah. I guess it is."

I stepped out of the back room. "Did Steve call yet?"

No one answered. I checked my watch. It was ten after six. "How long does it take to look at a body and see if it is Francine or not?"

It was another twenty minutes before my cell rang. When I saw it was Steve calling, my hands actually shook. "This is it."

Chapter Nineteen

I ANSWERED MY cell. "Hello?"

"Glinda. It's Steve. Once more, I have to say I am impressed."

My knees almost buckled. "It worked?"

"It worked. Would you and your gang be willing to return to the station where we can chat? I received a call from the phone company about a few things. We have Patricia dead to rights."

I actually jumped up and down. "We'll be there." I spun around. "It worked!"

Once everyone finished cheering, we closed the store and headed down the street to the sheriff's office. I didn't see Francine or Patricia, but most likely those two ladies were in the cells in back. I bet they weren't having a pleasant time being next to each other.

Steve greeted us in front and escorted us to the conference room. We all sat down while he remained standing.

"For starters, the phone company got back to me. They were able to identify that Elizabeth received both creepy phone calls from Patricia Haltern's phone. Unfortunately, we were unable to learn what was said.

That gave me an idea. "I hear there is software that allows

you to record your calls." I looked over at Jaxson. "We should get that for the future."

"For sure. The problem is remembering to turn it on."

That was so true. "Sorry to interrupt, Steve."

"No problem." Steve turned to Rihanna. "Your friend Casi would be proud of her brother. Christian did an admirable acting job in convincing Patricia to check out Francine's body. She wanted to see Francine so much that he didn't have to put a spell on Patricia."

Rihanna smiled. "I'll be sure to tell her. What was Christian's response?"

"His response?"

"Casi always felt that her brother just needed to be given a chance to be good. He's smart and talented but quite unlucky."

Jaxson cleared his throat. "Sounds like me, until I met Glinda."

"Thank you." I rubbed his arm.

Steve cleared his throat. "If you're asking if I might use him again for a sting operation, the answer is a strong maybe."

I liked that about Steve. He was open-minded. "What happened when Patricia arrived at the morgue?"

"I have her on tape, but the short of it was that she not only believed it was Francine, but she said a few things to indicate she was happy Francine was dead."

"Did she confess to calling me and asking me to kill her?" Elizabeth asked.

"No. I'm afraid not."

"Will she get any time?" Andorra asked.

"That will depend on Elizabeth and Christian. There

should be enough evidence to prove she blackmailed Elizabeth into performing a spell—which thankfully Elizabeth never did. We have Patricia on video paying Christian to kidnap—or rather mind-control—Andorra. I certainly can attest to Andorra's mental condition when she returned. That probably won't hold up in court, but we might try her in another court, one that will understand."

I loved it. Only then did it occur to me to ask about the old lady in the morgue. "Did Elissa say if the body returned to her old self?"

"She hasn't called yet, but I would consider that a good thing. I'm sure if she looks like Francine tomorrow, you all will be getting a call from a not-so-happy medical examiner."

Drake pushed back his chair. "I, too, want to thank everyone here for helping to bring justice for Kyle. It would have made him proud to know so many cared about him."

"Not that it really matters now," I said, "but did the lab get back to you, Steve, about the contents of the punch bowl?"

"Funny you should ask. They did, but the results were rather strange. The punch was not poisoned, but what Kyle drank was. It's almost like someone doused his drink, yet no one got near him after he poured the drink."

"There's no mystery to that," I said. "The extra ingredient in his cup is what converted the rather benign ingredients to something deadly."

"What extra ingredient?"

"Magic."

He flashed me a smile and shook his head. "I should have known."

Since all of the loose ends were now tied up, we left the

station. Elizabeth and Andorra could return home since Patricia was in jail. "Lock your door, ladies. I don't trust Patricia's husband. He can't be happy that his wife was so enamored with another man after all these years that she'd try to murder Kyle's killer. Harry might want revenge, assuming he knows who was involved in bringing her down." Or was I just being paranoid? That was most likely the case. Stress often messed with my mind.

Drake nodded. "If that is the case, how about both of you staying with me another night? I'll check to make sure he's left town."

The cousins looked at each other and nodded. Somehow, I got the sense Andorra agreed not because she feared for her safety but for other reasons. Go, Drake!

A LITTLE BEFORE one in the afternoon, Jaxson knocked on my apartment door. I knew it was him from the strength of his knock. Plus, that was when he told me he'd pick me up. Going to funerals was not my favorite pastime, but I wanted to be there for Drake.

I opened the door and inhaled. "Wow. You look…amazing."

Sure, I'd seen him in a suit before, but this black one fit him really well. He stepped inside and lightly kissed me. "You do, too. You are actually wearing black."

"I caved and bought a black dress." I'd even taken off my pink pendant since it looked a bit too festive. It was a hard decision since it had helped twice with the case. "How is

Drake doing?"

Jaxson shrugged. "He seems okay. While he is sad that Kyle's life was cut short, he is grateful that it brought him and Andorra together. I think he believes Kyle meant it to be."

I smiled. "It's a nice sentiment." I turned to Iggy. "Are you sure you don't want to come? After all you helped solve this case."

"Thanks, but no. I don't like dead bodies."

If Hugo had been able to go, I bet Iggy would have changed his mind. "I understand."

The temperature had turned warmer, and the sun was shining brightly. I pretended it was a tribute to Kyle Covington. When we stepped into the chapel, I expected there to be at most five people. To my amazement, the room was at least half full.

Jaxson leaned toward me. "I didn't think so many would show up."

"Me neither. Drake said Kyle didn't have that many friends in high school, but memories have a way of fading over the years."

I recognized a few from my class. The rest were probably significant others. We slipped in next to Drake, Andorra, and Elizabeth. In front of us was Jude. He turned around and nodded.

When I spotted Kim Lucas, the head of the reunion committee, I understood why so many were there. She'd probably called each and every one of them.

By the time the service began, the place was almost completely full. I had no idea what Kyle's parents looked like, but I didn't see anyone who fit the bill. They said they'd make it, but time had run out, and my heart broke.

The preacher stood, spoke briefly about Kyle, and then asked for others to make a comment.

It came as no surprise that both Jude and Drake spoke with fondness about their friend and his accomplishments. What I didn't expect, was how many of the others said something, recounting positive stories about Kyle's life.

About a third of the way through the service, the doors burst open, and it was as if the air left the room. Everyone turned around.

"They made it!" Drake said.

Thank goodness. He and Jude jumped up and worked their way back to them. Jude hugged Kyle's mom. After a brief discussion, he led them to the front row. Kyle's father then walked up to the podium.

Tears brimmed his eyes. "I am still in shock over the number of people here, but I'm so grateful. I'm sorry my wife and I were late, but we were on a cruise in the Mediterranean when we received the news of our son's death. It took everyone helping to get us off that boat and in to a port. We haven't slept in two days, so forgive us if I don't make a lot of sense. I'm not sure what has or hasn't been said, but your presence here means everything to us. His mom and I loved our son very much. Kyle will be missed more than you can know."

With his head bowed, he left the altar and sat next to his wife.

Apparently, no one wanted to follow that heart wrenching message, so the priest finished the sermon. One by one, we went up to the parents and spoke to them.

Once the service concluded, it seemed as if life could return to normal. Jude would be flying back to California tomorrow—alone. Jaxson and I went up to him. "I'm sorry we had to meet under these circumstances. Have you figured out your next move?" I asked.

"I have. I've reached out to Ronnie. I think with a little coaxing, I can convince him to join me in running the company."

"That's wonderful," I said.

"I'll have the not so fun chore of finding another accountant, however. This time, I think I'll go with a male."

That made me smile. After a quick goodbye, Jaxson and I headed back to my place. Iggy would want the rundown. On the way upstairs, I grabbed a few cookies to go. We debated stopping at the tea or coffee shop, but with the number of alums still in town, we thought it best to wait until the crowd thinned.

Once in my apartment, I poured myself some iced tea and made Jaxson a cup of coffee.

"I've been thinking," he said, as he pulled out a chair in the kitchen.

"About?"

"We've been working hard and haven't had a vacation in a long time."

My pulse soared. A vacation? Since he'd used the word *we*, it implied he wanted us to go together, which sounded serious. "Where do you have in mind?"

"In my ideal world, I'd have a passport, and if I did, I'd suggest a cruise to Italy."

I chuckled. "In your dreams."

Iggy was on the kitchen counter. "I want to go to Italy."

I patted his head. "I'm not sure they'd appreciate you there. Iguanas might even be a delicacy." Yes, that was a lie, but I couldn't help myself.

My familiar turned to Jaxson. "Tell me she's making that up."

My boyfriend betrayed me. "Yes, she is, but remember, where we go, you go."

Jaxson was hopeless. Iggy had wrapped him around his little finger. "Do you have a destination in mind?" I asked.

"Someplace warm and welcoming. I was thinking we could spend a few days in the Florida Keys."

I pulled out the remaining chair and sat down. I lifted his hands and squeezed. "I would love nothing more."

"I intend to swim and sunbathe, as well as sightsee. You up for it?"

"I would go anywhere with you, Jaxson Harrison."

He pushed back his chair, stood, and drew me to my feet. The kiss that followed confirmed that he was the man who'd stolen my heart.

I hope you enjoyed The Poisoned Pink Punch. As soon as I introduced Hugo, I knew I had to have him be part of the Witch's Cove family. Besides, I didn't want Iggy to be sad.

What's next? Someone burns down the bookstore, and it soon becomes evident that magic is involved. Did you expect anything less? Don't worry Hugo and Iggy join forces to stop the arsonist.

Buy on Amazon or read for FREE on Kindle Unlimited

Don't forget to sign up for my Cozy Mystery newsletter *to learn about my discounts and upcoming releases. If you prefer to only receive notices regarding my releases, follow me on BookBub.*
http://smarturl.it/VellaDayNL
bookbub.com/authors/vella-day

Here is a sneak peak of book 11: **Pink Smoke and Mirrors**

IGGY'S SMALL ANIMAL claws scraped down my face, rousing me from slumber. "Glinda, wake up," he said.

It took a second to realize that my pink familiar was on my bed—in my space. I cracked open an eye, expecting sunlight to be pouring into the room. Instead, darkness surrounded me. I might have rolled over and ignored my iguana, except that Iggy never woke me in the middle of the night without cause.

When my brain finally engaged, I jerked awake. "What is

it?"

"I smell smoke."

"In the apartment?" I don't know why I asked. Smoke was smoke. I inhaled but detected nothing.

"No. It's outside. Something's on fire down the street."

My pulse sped up. I could have asked him which building was ablaze, but I wanted to see for myself. I threw off the covers and raced to the window. Pink smoke was billowing from the rooftop of some building down the street, only I couldn't be certain which one it was. And why the pink color?

A blaring siren raced toward town from the north. Good. The fire department was coming. Heart racing, I flipped on the overhead light, pulled off my pajamas, and tossed on some clothes.

"Can I come with you?" Iggy asked.

"Your lungs can't take the smoke." Mine probably couldn't either, but I could protect myself better.

"Take pictures."

"It's pitch black. Sit on the ledge and watch. You won't miss a thing."

He waddled over to the window, and I lifted him onto the sill, even though he could climb up by himself.

I grabbed a sweater in case it was chilly, but if there was fire, I imagine I wouldn't need one. I could only hope this was a kitchen fire and not something more sinister, but at four in the morning, I wasn't holding my breath for a good outcome.

I ran down the staircase and out the side entrance to the alleyway that separated the Tiki Hut Grill where my apartment was located and the Cove Mortuary that my parents owned.

As soon as I made it to the main street, the sheriff's car pulled in front of...oh, no...Candle's Bookstore. That was one of Witch's Cove's icons. I'd bought books there since I was a kid.

Along with the Jaxson Harrison, I ran the Pink Iguana Sleuths agency, and I'd be using all my sleuthing and witch abilities to find out who did this—assuming it was arson and not caused by faulty wiring or something. That was a possibility since the building was rather ancient.

When I made it across the street, our deputy, Nash Solano, stopped me. "You can't get any closer, Glinda. It's not safe."

I couldn't see any flames or feel the heat. The entire interior appeared to be filled with pink smoke, though. "What's going on?"

"I'd like to ask you that."

"Me?" He couldn't think that because pink was my signature color that I was involved in this.

"Why are you out here in the middle of the night?" he asked.

"Iggy woke me up saying he smelled smoke. That motivated me to get out of bed, and when I spotted the pink color, I couldn't help but investigate." I clasped his arm. "You don't think I had anything to do with this, do you? You have to know that I love this bookstore."

"I can't say one way or another."

Couldn't or wouldn't? Just then one of the firefighters motioned that he needed to speak with Nash, giving me a moment to observe what was going on—which wasn't much. The two of them chatted for a moment and then Nash returned. "Excuse me, Glinda, but duty calls. Please go home. There is nothing to see or do here."

Easy for him to say. I should have let Iggy come with me. He could have cloaked himself and then listened in on their conversation without being detected. But alas, Iggy was watching from my bedroom window. Not wanting to be hauled in for being a suspected arsonist, I headed back across the street.

By now, two or three other folks had come to gawk. Considering a small group was gathering, with probably more to come, tomorrow would be soon enough to find out what happened. Since no ambulance had arrived, and none of the adjacent stores seemed to have been harmed, there probably was nothing for me to do—at least not tonight.

No surprise, when I returned to the apartment, Iggy was pacing the living room.

"Well?" he asked.

"There's not much to tell other than the bookstore is filled with smoke. If I had to guess, I'd say the back room caught on fire."

"I thought smoke was gray."

"It is. Frank must have kept some chemicals back there that caused the pink color." Why a bookstore owner would have chemicals was anyone's guess. I yawned. "I'm sure by tomorrow, the town will be abuzz with what happened. I'm going to try to get some shuteye. I suggest you do the same."

I headed toward my bedroom, happy that Iggy seemed content to leave the questions until morning. Unfortunately, it wasn't long before a knock sounded on my apartment door. Because it wasn't a strong sound, I assumed it was my Aunt

Fern who lived across the hall come to check on me—or rather to give me the latest update since she was one of the main gossip queens in town. My aunt owned the Tiki Hut Grill, along with the two apartments that resided above it, and she had probably learned what had happened last night.

I swung my legs over the bed, but before I had the chance to stand, my aunt came into my bedroom.

"Excuse the intrusion," she said. "Iggy crawled out of the cat door and gave me your keys so I could let myself in."

I'd given her a spare key, but she must have forgotten. "No problem. I trust you heard about the fire at the bookstore?" I asked.

I scooted over on the bed and patted the space next to me. She sat down. "Of course, I did. Pearl called me. How did you hear about it?"

Being close to eighty, Pearl Dillsmith was the oldest of the local gossip queens. She also was the sheriff's dispatcher as well as his grandmother.

"After Iggy smelled the smoke around four in the morning, I checked it out, but I couldn't see much. Did you get the deets on what happened?"

"From what I heard, no one was injured, but between the fire hoses and the sprinklers, all of the books were ruined."

My heart ached for Frank and Betty Sanchez. They'd run that store for as long as I could remember. "How terrible. Did Steve have any idea what happened?"

Pearl probably knew everything her grandson did, and if she knew, the town's gossips knew. "It was arson," my aunt said.

I sucked in a breath. "Arson? I was actually hoping the

microwave in back had short-circuited or something."

Aunt Fern lifted her chin. "Want to know what I think?"

"Always."

"I think Frank set the fire himself."

I barked out a laugh. "Seriously? Why? That bookstore is his life."

"There are many reasons. The first is that he is in his seventies, and he wants to retire."

That was lame. "He could sell his inventory and the goodwill that goes with it. Burning it down is rather extreme."

My aunt shook her head. "He's been renting the space all these years and is behind in his rent payments, or so I've heard. Don't you remember when Betty told you that she and Frank had asked their son for money to help them out?"

"Yes, but he turned them down, or so she claimed. No one was able to corroborate that request, though." Her son, Daniel Sanchez, had been a wealthy lawyer in Miami who was murdered shortly after that conversation.

She shrugged. "I imagine they still owe money to Heath Richards, the building's new owner."

"How does ruining your business help you pay your bills?" I didn't want to think Frank was guilty of anything.

"Insurance money."

"They won't pay if Frank set the fire."

Aunt Fern painted on her Mona Lisa smile. "You don't know?"

Clearly, I must not. "Know what?"

"Frank Sanchez was the fire chief some twenty or thirty years ago. He would know how to cover his tracks."

"What? Bookstore owner Frank Sanchez was the fire

chief? How did I not know this?"

My aunt clasped my hand. "You were merely a child back then."

"Why did he quit?" I don't know why it mattered now, though.

"I don't recall."

Uh-huh. Sure, she didn't. My aunt remembered everything—except that I'd given her my spare key. Not to worry, there were others who would spill the beans. "Thanks for the update."

My aunt stood. "I'd hate for it to be Frank. I really do. That means you and Jaxson need to find out who did this."

"I'll give it my best." And I would, too.

Once she left, I redressed and then headed over to the office. If Jaxson hadn't picked up any chatter about the fire, we'd stop over at the diner, the tea shop, or the coffee shop to see what the other gossip queens had to say. The fire—or smoke bomb—happened five hours ago. Surely, that was enough time for people to spread the word about who might have been responsible.

When Iggy and I arrived at the office, my eighteen-year old cousin, Rihanna, had already left for school, leaving Jaxson alone at his desk. He turned around. "I trust you heard about the fire?"

"I sure did." I explained how Iggy had woken me up in the middle of the night, and how I'd rushed over to investigate.

"Learn anything?"

Considering the website he had up showed pink smoke, he'd heard about that aspect of the crime. "Not much other than Aaron Reed appeared to be first on the scene."

"Aaron, huh? What did he have to say?"

Aaron graduated a year ahead of Jaxson. I didn't know many of Jaxson's classmates since he was six years older than me, but he'd mentioned Aaron a few times. The man had been trouble, almost as much as Jaxson himself.

"He was busy chatting with Nash. I don't think he saw me."

"The two of us might have to have a talk—for old times' sake, of course."

"I didn't think you liked each other," I said.

Jaxson huffed. "Kids like us didn't like anyone. I think we respected each other, though, since we both disregarded the rules back then."

"What made him change?" Jaxson wasn't the same person after he'd been accused of robbing a liquor store and then had to spend three years in jail before finally being acquitted. Thankfully, our former sheriff finally admitted he'd trumped up the charges to avoid accusing his son.

"Who's to say he is any different now?"

"He's a fireman. Police and firemen are civil servants. They are supposed to be noble."

His chuckle sounded rueful. "If I recall, the past sheriff and deputy of Witch's Cove were civil servants, and they were as corrupt as they came."

"That's true." One was dead and the other was in jail. Time to get back to business. I nodded to the screen. "Whatcha got there."

"I was curious about the pink smoke."

"Me, too. Nash kind of joked about it having to do with

me."

Jackson shook his head. "I'm sure he was kidding."

"I hope so, unless someone is trying to frame me. I don't think I've made that many enemies, except for maybe all the people I've helped put behind bars."

He chuckled. "Let's explore that idea last." He tapped the screen. "It says here that pink smoke can be caused by the chemical, lithium chloride. It's used in smoke bombs to create the pink color."

"And if a smoke bomb was involved, can one of those even do much harm?"

"I don't know. It also says here that this chemical is used in auto repair for welding. The article then gives a bunch of chemical nonsense that I don't understand. Chemistry wasn't my best subject."

"I loved science, but maybe Christian Durango can help us."

"Because he is an auto mechanic?"

I shrugged. "Can't hurt to ask. He helped with our last case." His sister, who was fast becoming one of Rihanna's best friends, said his attitude toward life had improved quite a lot after being thought of in a positive light for a change.

"Let's talk to him. If nothing else, Christian might be able to ask around to see who has some of this chemical."

We headed over to the garage where Christian worked. He and I had graduated in the same class, yet until one of our fellow classmates had been murdered last month, I hadn't seen Christian in years.

It took less than ten minutes to reach his garage. "Let's hope he is working today."

"If not, I bet the boss can help us."

"True."

We parked and went inside where we found Christian changing the oil in a car.

"Hey, Christian," I tried to sound upbeat.

He spun around. For a moment, he looked as if he'd seen a ghost. "What are you guys doing here?" He seemed cautious yet friendly.

"Did you hear about the fire at Candle's Bookstore?"

"No. I don't get into town much. What happened?"

I explained about the smoke I saw.

"What does that have to do with me?" This time his defenses had shot up.

Poor guy must have been wrongfully accused quite often in the past to have that kind of reaction.

Jaxson stepped forward. "I did some research. The smoke might have been caused by some lithium chloride igniting."

Christian whistled. "I've never used that stuff, but another one of our auto repair guys has. We use it as a brazing flux for aluminum, but it can be used for a lot of other repair work, too. I even heard it can be used as a drying agent for dehumidifiers. You'd have to ask a chemistry guy for the specifics."

The more ways to use it, the harder it would be to pin down who might have any. "Do you think we can speak with this other mechanic?"

"Glen's not in yet, but when he gets here, I can ask him about it and get back to you."

"Sounds great." This could be the lead we needed.

"Is that all?"

I nodded. "For now."

"Let me know if I can help in any way," Christian said.

How cool was it that he seemed to want to work with us again? "We will."

Since we learned the information we'd come for, Jaxson and I left. "He isn't telling us everything," Jaxson said as we headed to his truck.

"Why would you say that? I know Rihanna can read minds. Can you do that now?"

"Hardly, but he had a hard time making eye contact."

"Maybe he's used to having people think the worst of him. Are you suggesting Christian had something to do with the burning of the bookstore?"

"Maybe, maybe not, but he is a warlock, don't forget."

"I bet he hasn't been in that store in ten years."

"Who's to say someone didn't hire him to use magic to set off a pink bomb and then light the fire?"

Jaxson's imagination was out of control. To be fair, Christian had used his warlock skills recently for no good. "I'd love to find out if a person with magical abilities could even do that, because if he can, I want to learn that trick."

Jaxson smiled. "That's my girl."

I wasn't sure what he meant by that, but I hoped he was just teasing me.

Buy on Amazon or read for FREE on Kindle Unlimited

THE END

A WITCH'S COVE MYSTERY (Paranormal Cozy Mystery)
PINK Is The New Black (book 1)
A PINK Potion Gone Wrong (book 2)
The Mystery of the PINK Aura (book 3)
Box Set (books 1-3)
Sleuthing In The PINK (book 4)
Not in The PINK (book 5)
Gone in the PINK of an Eye (book 6)
Box Set (books 4-6)
The PINK Pumpkin Party (book 7)
Mistletoe with a PINK Bow (book 8)
The Magical PINK Pendant (book 9)
The Poisoned PINK Punch (book 10)
PINK Smoke and Mirrors (book 11)
Broomsticks and PINK Gumdrops (book 12)
Knotted Up In PINK Yarn (book 13)

SILVER LAKE SERIES (3 OF THEM)
(1). HIDDEN REALMS OF SILVER LAKE
(Paranormal Romance)
Awakened By Flames (book 1)
Seduced By Flames (book 2)
Kissed By Flames (book 3)
Destiny In Flames (book 4)
Box Set (books 1-4)
Passionate Flames (book 5)
Ignited By Flames (book 6)
Touched By Flames (book 7)
Box Set (books 5-7)
Bound By Flames (book 8)

Fueled By Flames (book 9)
Scorched By Flames (book 10)

(2). **FOUR SISTERS OF FATE: HIDDEN REALMS OF SILVER LAKE** (Paranormal Romance)

Poppy (book 1)
Primrose (book 2)
Acacia (book 3)
Magnolia (book 4)
Box Set (books 1-4)
Jace (book 5)
Tanner (book 6)

(3). **WERES AND WITCHES OF SILVER LAKE**
(Paranormal Romance)

A Magical Shift (book 1)
Catching Her Bear (book 2)
Surge of Magic (book 3)
The Bear's Forbidden Wolf (book 4)
Her Reluctant Bear (book 5)
Freeing His Tiger (book 6)
Protecting His Wolf (book 7)
Waking His Bear (book 8)
Melting Her Wolf's Heart (book 9)
Her Wolf's Guarded Heart (book 10)
His Rogue Bear (book 11)
Box Set (books 1-4)
Box Set (books 5-8)
Reawakening Their Bears (book 12)

OTHER PARANORMAL SERIES

PACK WARS (Paranormal Romance)
Training Their Mate (book 1)
Claiming Their Mate (book 2)
Rescuing Their Virgin Mate (book 3)
Box Set (books 1-3)
Loving Their Vixen Mate (book 4)
Fighting For Their Mate (book 5)
Enticing Their Mate (book 6)
Box Set (books 1-4)
Complete Box Set (books 1-6)

HIDDEN HILLS SHIFTERS (Paranormal Romance)
An Unexpected Diversion (book 1)
Bare Instincts (book 2)
Shifting Destinies (book 3)
Embracing Fate (book 4)
Promises Unbroken (book 5)
Bare 'N Dirty (book 6)
Hidden Hills Shifters Complete Box Set (books 1-6)

CONTEMPORARY SERIES
MONTANA PROMISES
(Full length contemporary Romance)
Promises of Mercy (book 1)
Foundations For Three (book 2)
Montana Fire (book 3)
Montana Promises Box Set (books 1-3)
Hart To Hart (Book 4)
Burning Seduction (Book 5)
Montana Promises Complete Box Set (books 1-5)

ROCK HARD, MONTANA

(contemporary romance novellas)

Montana Desire (book 1)

Awakening Passions (book 2)

PLEDGED TO PROTECT

(contemporary romantic suspense)

From Panic To Passion (book 1)

From Danger To Desire (book 2)

From Terror To Temptation (book 3)

Pledged To Protect Box Set (books 1-3)

BURIED SERIES (contemporary romantic suspense)

Buried Alive (book 1)

Buried Secrets (book 2)

Buried Deep (book 3)

The Buried Series Complete Box Set (books 1-3)

A NASH MYSTERY (Contemporary Romance)

Sidearms and Silk(book 1)

Black Ops and Lingerie(book 2)

A Nash Mystery Box Set (books 1-2)

STARTER SETS (Romance)

Contemporary

Paranormal

Author Bio

Love it HOT and STEAMY? Sign up for my newsletter and receive MONTANA DESIRE for FREE. smarturl.it/o4cz93?IQid=MLite

OR Are you a fan of quirky PARANORMAL COZY MYSTERIES? Sign up for this newsletter. smarturl.it/CozyNL

Not only do I love to read, write, and dream, I'm an extrovert. I enjoy being around people and am always trying to understand what makes them tick. Not only must my romance books have a happily ever after, I need characters I can relate to. My men are wonderful, dynamic, smart, strong, and the best lovers in the world (of course).

My Paranormal Cozy Mysteries are where I let my imagination run wild with witches and a talking pink iguana who believes he's a real sleuth.

I believe I am the luckiest woman. I do what I love and I have a wonderful, supportive husband, who happens to be hot!

Fun facts about me

(1) I'm a math nerd who loves spreadsheets. Give me numbers and I'll find a pattern.

(2) I live on a Costa Rica beach!

(3) I also like to exercise. Yes, I know I'm odd.

I love hearing from readers either on FB or via email (hint, hint).

Social Media Sites

Website:
www.velladay.com

FB:
facebook.com/vella.day.90

Twitter:
@velladay4

Gmail:
velladayauthor@gmail.com

Printed in Great Britain
by Amazon

58178458R00125